# So Long,
## Jackie Robinson

# So Long, Jackie Robinson

## Nancy L. M. Russell

KEY PORTER BOOKS

**Library and Archives Canada Cataloguing in Publication**

Russell, Nancy L. M. (Nancy Leigh Mary), 1963-
    So long, Jackie Robinson / Nancy Russell.

ISBN 978-1-55263-863-7

    1. Robinson, Jackie, 1919-1972–Juvenile fiction. 2. Montreal Royals (Baseball team)–Juvenile fiction. I. Title.

PS8585.U774S6 2007        jC813'.54        C2006-906437-7 2

The publisher gratefully acknowledges the support of the Canada Council for the Arts and the Ontario Arts Council for its publishing program. We acknowledge the support of the Government of Ontario through the Ontario Media Development Corporation's Ontario Book Initiative.

We acknowledge the financial support of the Government of Canada through the Book Publishing Industry Development Program (BPIDP) for our publishing activities.

Key Porter Books Limited
Six Adelaide Street East, Tenth Floor
Toronto, Ontario
Canada  M5C 1H6

www.keyporter.com

Text design and electronic formatting: Martin Gould

Printed and bound in Canada

07 08 09 10 11 5 4 3 2 1

"A life is not important except in the impact it has on other lives."
—*Epitaph on Jackie Robinson's headstone*

# Author's Note

Some of the language used to describe Jackie Robinson and the other African-American characters in the book is dated and even derogatory. In 1946, when this story is set, African-Americans were referred to as "coloured" or "Negroes." Racists called them "niggers." These words are all unacceptable by today's standards. Jackie Robinson did his part to help change that.

To find out more about Jackie Robinson, I recommend *Baseball's Great Experiment* by Jules Tygiel, *Jackie Robinson: A Biography* by Arnold Rampersad and *Great Time Coming,* by David Falkner. I have borrowed liberally from these books and other sources to recreate what it was like to live in this ground-breaking time in Montreal. I have taken some historical licence to bring Jackie's world to life.

# So Long,
## Jackie Robinson

Prologue

# The Beginning

## Montreal Signs Negro Player

*Montreal, October 23, 1945*

The first Negro player ever to be admitted to organized baseball was signed tonight by the Brooklyn Dodgers for their International League farm club, the Montreal Royals.

"Jack Robinson is a fine type of young man, intelligent and college bred, and I think he can take it, too," said Branch Rickey, president of the Dodgers, in making the announcement.

## Robinson: I'm Just a Guinea Pig

*Montreal, November 1, 1945*

"Guess I'm just a guinea pig in this noble experiment," said Jack Robinson, the Negro player signed by the Montreal Royals.

"If I can make good here, with this Montreal club, which is likely the only club where I might have been given this chance," said Robinson, "then it will be a new deal for men of my race."

## Chapter One

# The Ballpark

THE FIRST THING HE HEARD was the crack of a ball against a wooden baseball bat. Matthew Parker froze in his tracks. He had been trudging along a sidewalk that was just warming up in the spring sunshine. In his left hand, he carried a stick that made a rat-a-tat sound against the iron railing that lined the row of houses along the downtown Montreal street.

It had been three weeks since he'd heard a bat and ball.

"Not since I got dragged out here," he muttered bitterly to himself. He thought about his baseball glove, gathering dust in the apartment he shared with his mother and new stepfather. Before he left Pembroke, not a day would go by that he didn't put on his glove. Even in the coldest days of winter, he always took comfort from the familiar feel and wonderful smell of the soft leather. Baseball meant summer and friendship and home. At least it used to.

Matthew tried to keep in touch with the world of major league baseball as best he could. He'd often huddle next to the radio in the kitchen of their small third-floor apartment. And he'd sneak the sports section from Alain's newspapers whenever he could. Alain was trying to learn English, so he had the Gazette and sometimes even the *Globe and Mail*. Of course, Alain also picked up the Quebec tabloids, jam-packed with articles about hockey. Matthew would try his best to decipher the stories and statistics in the French ones. He didn't want to come out and ask his stepfather to borrow them, though. That would mean having to speak to the person who had ruined his life.

It was early April now—almost a month since they'd left Pembroke—and Matthew was still learning his way around Montreal. Even now, standing still in the middle of the sidewalk with a stick in his hand, Matthew had no real idea where he was. All he knew was that someone somewhere was playing baseball. Suddenly, the distant sound of a public address system crackled across the air and reached his ears. Matthew's feet began to move instinctively, drawing him closer to the source of the noise. As he walked, stick held quietly in his hand, he could have sworn that he heard again the familiar *thwack* of a wooden bat hitting a ball.

This was the farthest he had dared to go from his

apartment building. The neighbourhood where they lived was filled with French-Canadian families who loved to sit out on their wrought iron balconies or front stoops. Matthew always kept his head down and eyes on the ground as he walked past the row of houses. He spoke very little French, and was petrified that if someone spoke to him he'd be unable to reply. As he walked past a neighbourhood bakery, Matthew slowed to breathe in the smell of the freshly baked loaves of bread called "baguettes." Next, he passed a little grocery store, jammed to the rafters with canned goods and other supplies. The war had ended only last fall, so everyone was still limited to their rations. Even so, it seemed to Matthew that Montrealers had plenty of stores and restaurants, especially compared to Pembroke.

Another crack of the bat! Matthew moved past the apartments and stores until he could see a large factory—complete with a water tower and smoke stack—ahead in the distance. On top of the building, in large letters, was a sign that said, "Knit to Fit." He laughed—and then looked around to make sure nobody had heard him.

Matthew turned a corner and, suddenly, there it was—a large, red brick stadium. He dropped his stick as he hurried toward one of the many entrances. Desperate for a look inside, Matthew leaned on a chain-link door. To his surprise, the door swung open, and, after a quick look, Matthew scurried through the opening and into a gate that led to the bleachers.

It was a ballpark—the biggest Matthew had ever seen. He caught his breath as he gazed around the stadium, soaking in all the sights and sounds. The field was like a glistening green lake, reflecting the late afternoon sun. The lush green grass was trimmed to perfection and the white markings glimmered in the sunlight. Enormous green walls flanked either side of the field. On one side, he recognized the smokestack and the Knit to Fit factory's sign. A giant scoreboard filled the outfield wall, with colourful cigarette and candy ads on either side.

Rows of blue metal seats reached up to the sky. The bleachers at the far sides of home plate were open to the elements, but the upper rows were covered by an overhang. Matthew looked up to the very top of the stadium and gave a low whistle.

"That would be some view," he said aloud. There was still no one around, so he made his way slowly out of the gate and along the edge of the field toward home plate.

Matthew looked up again. From his new position, he could see a row of windows in the stands high above home plate. He remembered reading that newspaper and radio reporters had their own area of the ballpark so they could sit and type their stories during the game. Then, he remembered something else. The Montreal

Royals! This stadium had to be their home—it was too big and impressive to be a neighbourhood park. And, if so, this was where Jackie Robinson was going to play.

The Montreal papers were full of stories about the new Negro player who had been signed by the Royals, a Triple-A franchise in the International League. Even though he knew a lot about baseball, Matthew had never heard of the Royals, at least not until they'd signed Robinson the previous fall. That been big news everywhere, even in Pembroke.

Although Matthew didn't quite understand everything he'd read, he did know there was something very special about Robinson's arrival in Montreal. Not everyone, for example, seemed to think it was a good idea to have a Negro ballplayer in the big leagues. Matthew had no idea why.

"A.J. is never going to believe this." Matthew felt a pang of sadness as he thought of his best friend back home in Pembroke. He had no one to share in the excitement of this moment—seeing a big-league ballpark for the very first time. A dream come true in the midst of his otherwise miserable life. He sighed. It was time to go; his mother would be starting to worry.

Just as Matthew turned to walk away, a crowd of people approached from the other end of the field. In the middle of the crowd was a ballplayer, dressed in the blue-and-white uniform of the Montreal Royals. The player's face looked familiar, and Matthew caught his breath as he realized why. That face had been on the cover of every newspaper in the city for the past couple of weeks. The man in the middle of the crowd was none other than Jackie Robinson.

## Chapter Two

# Jackie Robinson

RIGHT BEFORE MATTHEW'S EYES, the ballpark came to life. Several players in uniform jogged out from an opening near the dugout. They were chewing and spitting tobacco, and casually chatting as they effortlessly swung their bats, preparing for their turn in the batting cage. Matthew recognized the stylized "Montreal" on their jerseys. More Royals!

Matthew made his way carefully through the grandstand to a corner where a crowd of reporters and photographers had gathered. Flash bulbs popped and voices rang out as Robinson and his crowd—mostly men in suits—walked toward the group.

One of the men in suits held up his arms, signalling for quiet.

"Gentlemen, please. Mr. Robinson only has about fifteen minutes before batting practice but he'll try to answer as many of your questions as possible."

"What did you think of your reception in the United States?"

"How did it feel to get that home run in your first game in Jersey City?"

"What do you think of Canada so far? Is it different from the States?"

Matthew stood quietly behind the crowd, straining to get a closer look at the man at the centre of all the attention.

Jackie Robinson was bigger in real life, Matthew thought, than he appeared in the newspapers. He probably weighed about two hundred pounds and had a broad face and big hands—hands that were nervously clutching a bat and glove. His skin was the darkest Matthew had ever seen.

Matthew had never met a coloured person until his train trip to Montreal this spring. On trains, it seemed, almost all of the porters were black. There certainly weren't any coloured people in Pembroke, and the black ballplayer was the first one he'd actually seen here in Montreal.

Jackie Robinson towered over most of the reporters. On his head, he wore a ball cap with the letter "M" at the centre. His jersey was carefully tucked into his pants, and the belt was pulled tight at his waist. His pants ballooned over his thick muscular legs, then narrowed at the shins, where he wore his socks neatly pulled up to his knees.

Robinson answered all the reporters' questions in a

quiet, deliberate tone, choosing his words carefully. Matthew was surprised by Robinson's voice. He had expected a deep bass from such a big man; instead, Jackie's voice was quite high and gentle.

Robinson told the reporters he was pleased with his debut in the International League. It sure felt good, he said, to hit that home run in his first-ever professional game.

"And my wife, Rachel, and I are feeling very welcome here in Montreal," Robinson added, with a toothy smile. "We don't speak any French, but everyone is trying to make us feel right at home."

"What was it like on opening day in New Jersey?" shouted a young reporter, who then held up his camera and flashed another photo.

"Well, I must admit I had a lump in my throat as I listened to the national anthem," Robinson said, turning to face the young man. "My heart was beating fast and I could feel a few butterflies. It was 3:04, I remember, when I got up to the bat," he continued. Some of the writers were hanging on his every word; others were scribbling frantically in their notebooks. "The crowd gave me a little cheer ... that felt good. I worked the pitcher to a full count, then had a weak grounder right at the shortstop. It wasn't much of a swing," Robinson chuckled, "but it helped with the butterflies."

"And what about that home run? How did that feel, Jackie?"

"That was in the third," Robinson recalled. "Two on and that pitcher was sure I was going to bunt. But I swung on a fastball hard and down the middle."

"That was hard all right," chuckled a burly man in a Royals uniform who stood at Robinson's elbow.

"Mr. Hopper, what did you think of Jackie's home run?" The question came from the middle of the pack. Matthew was finding it hard to keep up with who was asking what. The man in the suit jumped to answer.

"Boys, you all know Clay Hopper, the manager of the Royals, I'm sure." He then stepped back to let Hopper respond.

"It sure was swell," Hopper replied with a broad grin. "That ball went 340 feet into the left-field stands."

He shook his head at the memory. "Gentlemen, we have to wrap things up in just a moment," said Hopper. "It was one heckuva debut, with four hits, including a homer, two steals and four runs scored. We're happy to have him."

"What about the black cat in Syracuse?" The question was asked in a voice so soft that Matthew had trouble hearing.

"I'm here to talk about baseball," said Jackie, the smile disappearing from his face.

"That's enough questions for today." Hopper waved back the crowd and motioned for Jackie to join the other players. Before he left, Robinson shook hands with all the reporters. Then, he headed on to the field. As Matthew watched, Robinson trotted out to second base and starting tossing the ball around the infield with his teammates.

Matthew settled onto a bench in the front row of the stands, looking around carefully to make sure no one had noticed him. Thankfully, everyone was too busy watching Jackie Robinson to pay any attention to him.

He watched as the big man effortlessly threw the ball, dancing from one side of second base to the other. There wasn't much talking between the players now, who seemed suddenly serious compared to the playful banter that had taken place earlier around the batting cage. Everyone seemed very aware of all the cameras, chronicling their every move.

After some fielding drills, the players gathered around the cage. Without a word, Jackie picked up his bat and warmed up, waiting for his turn at the plate. He seemed oblivious to all the activity around him—totally focused on watching the pitcher and swinging his bat back and forth over his ample shoulders.

The reporters spread out behind the cage, grateful for the opportunity to talk with individual players as they waited to hit. Right in front of Matthew, a young fresh-faced reporter with a double-breasted suit and a hat shook hands with one of the Royals.

"I'm Tony Barton with the *Gazette*," the young writer

said. "But call me Dewey. Everyone does."

"Billy Marsden, backup catcher. You new here?" Marsden was a stocky man, and his uniform bulged at the waist. He constantly opened and closed the glove on his left hand as he spoke.

"Yup. Just moved here from Sault Ste. Marie, Ontario," the reporter answered. "I couldn't go overseas because of a bum knee, so I put in a couple of years with the home-town paper. But I've always dreamed of writing about pro sports, so here I am."

"Well, welcome to the big time," Billy replied. "Really big time, since Robinson arrived. I've never talked to this many reporters in my life."

"How do you think he's doing?" Dewey Barton asked, flipping open his notebook.

"He had a tough time in spring training," Marsden said, shaking his head. "You know, separate hotels—real rat-traps. And the crowds were not always the friend-liest. I've been around lots of ballparks in my time, but I've never heard some of the dirt that they were yelling at Jackie."

"Like what?" Dewey pressed for more details.

"Nigger comments," the player answered, reluctantly. "'Nigger go home.' 'No niggers in baseball.' All kinds of threats. Syracuse was the worst," Marsden continued. "One of the Chiefs' players, a real joker, tossed a black cat on to the field during the game. He said to Jackie,

'There's your cousin, boy.'"

"So that was the cat Jackie didn't want to talk about," Matthew thought as he moved a little closer. He wanted to hear more of what Marsden had to say.

"But Jackie got him back," the catcher continued. "He doubled to left, then scored on a single to centre. As he jogged in past the Syracuse dugout, Jackie said to the player, 'I guess my cousin's pretty happy now.'"

Marsden looked out at his fellow Royal, now up at the plate.

"How is Jackie taking it?" Dewey asked.

"I don't know how he does it," the catcher replied, shaking his head. "I've been around the International League for a while and I don't think I've ever seen anyone with the kind of guts he has. I mean, he gets a little edgy every once in a while, when the crowd's real mean," Marsden admitted. "But the next night, he bounces right back."

"His stats are sure good," agreed the young reporter. "A .372 batting average. Seventeen runs and eight stolen bases. Not bad at all!"

"He's taking it better than the rest of us would and plays better than the rest of us on top of it," Billy replied with a laugh. "He just does his job and then walks off the field. But you can tell just by the set of his shoulders that it gets to him sometimes."

"Do you think Branch Rickey knows what he's doing,

bringing Jackie to Montreal?" asked Barton. "Do you think Jackie Robinson will make it to the big leagues and break the colour barrier? Some folks say there's no way a Negro will ever be allowed to play in Brooklyn, even if that's where Mr. Rickey thinks he's heading."

Billy Marsden shrugged. "He's the boss, I guess. Jackie's doing okay so far, but I sure wouldn't want to be in his shoes."

Matthew's ears perked up at the mention of Branch Rickey. The general manager of the Brooklyn Dodgers was often featured in the sports sections. He'd caused quite a stir in bringing Jackie first to spring training and now here to Montreal. Some newspapermen had even dubbed Rickey's idea the "Great Experiment."

"You've been great, Billy. Can I talk to you again?" Dewey Barton asked eagerly, shaking the ballplayer's hand as Marsden prepared to take his turn at the plate.

"Sure thing. Good luck, kid," Billy answered, hustling onto the field.

# Chapter Three

# Dewey and Tyrone

### Robinson's Debut Ignites Royals' Fans
by Dewey Barton
*Montreal, April 19, 1946*

It is with incredible anticipation that the fans of the Montreal Royals await the home field debut of their new Negro player, Jackie Robinson. Robinson made his minor league debut yesterday at Jersey City's Roosevelt Stadium.

While many of us have pondered Branch Rickey's "Great Experiment" from afar, fifty thousand fans were there in person this historic afternoon to watch the twenty-seven-year-old Robinson in his first-ever professional outing.

DEWEY BARTON WAS STILL SCRIBBLING notes as he climbed into the stands and sat down just a few seats away from Matthew. The reporter stared out at the field, where Jackie Robinson was now standing at second base, practising double plays with one of the coaches. He had amazing grace for such a big man. As he repeated the drill over and over again, Robinson seemed determined to perfect it to his own satisfaction, even after the coach was ready to call it quits.

Barton paused in his note-taking, scanned the ball-park and squinted into the sun. A look of curiosity crossed his face as he noticed Matthew. The boy froze. It was finally going to happen. Someone was going to ask him to leave.

"*Il joue bien.*"

The reporter was talking to him. And even worse, he was speaking French. Matthew felt a wave of panic and couldn't think of a single word he had learned. What was he saying?

"Jackie Robinson? *Il joue bien,*" the reporter repeated with a kind smile.

Joue bien. Matthew knew that. Plays well. Okay, but what was he supposed to say back?

The reporter turned away and jotted a few more words in his notebook. Matthew desperately wanted to talk to him. But how?

"*Pardon moi,*" Matthew said tentatively, trying to catch the reporter's eye. "I, well, I don't speak French."

"Oh, shucks, me neither," the young man laughed. "My name's Tony Barton. From the *Gazette*. My friends call me Dewey."

"I'm Matthew Parker." They shook hands.

"You from Montreal, Matthew?"

"No, sir," Matthew replied. "I'm from Pembroke. My mother and I moved here a couple of weeks ago. She got married."

"Your pop in the army?" Dewey continued. He seemed genuinely interested.

Matthew nodded his head. "My real dad died in a car crash just after he and my mom were married. I never even knew him."

A shadow came over the reporter's face. "I lost my kid brother in the war."

He paused and looked around the ballpark, soaking it in. "Tommy was a big ball fan. He would have loved this."

Matthew wanted to tell Dewey more—about A.J. and about how his life had changed forever on the night Alain and Grace Parker met at the dancehall in Pembroke. Alain had been stationed there for his basic training and Grace was working in town as a secretary for a local law firm. Things had been fine, until she met Alain.

"How are you liking Montreal?" Dewey said, gently changing the subject. "It's quite a city, isn't it?"

"Yes, sir," Matthew replied, politely but with a noticeable lack of enthusiasm.

"What do you think of Jackie Robinson?" the reporter

continued. "He's something else, eh?"

"He sure is," Matthew replied, trying to get a closer look at Dewey's camera and notebook. "I'm a pitcher myself, sir."

"Oh, don't say sir! You make me feel old," Dewey laughed, giving Matthew a playful punch in the shoulder. "A pitcher, eh? Are you looking to crack the Royals' lineup then?"

A shadow crossed Matthew's face. "No, sir. I mean, no. I'm only twelve. And I don't even play ball anymore. Since we moved here to Montreal."

The two were interrupted by one of the cleaners, working his way through the stands. He was tall and sturdy and dressed in one of the ballpark jackets.

"I need to clean up now, boys."

The man's skin was as dark as Robinson's. Maybe even darker. His wiry, black hair was speckled with grey and there was a slight hunch to his shoulders, as if they'd seen plenty of hard work over the years. Matthew caught himself staring at the man's massive hands, gripping the broom and dust pan. His forearms and wrists were equally muscular. They seemed strangely young and powerful compared to the rest of the man's appearance.

"It's been some day, but it's time to go. We've got a big game comin' up." The man's voice rumbled in his chest as he spoke. He also sounded different—not like the porters on the train, not even like Jackie Robinson.

Matthew was curious. How had this man ended up at a ballpark in Montreal?

"What about you, sir? What do you think of Jackie Robinson?" Dewey picked up his notebook again, and pulled his pencil from behind his ear.

The man shook his head, laughing. "You don't care what ol' Tyrone thinks. No, sirree. I'm just a cleaner. The white folks don't care what I think."

"That's not true," Dewey persisted. "I care. Say, I may even have an angle here. What if I do a piece about you watching Jackie Robinson becoming the first Negro in baseball? Through the eyes of a black man at the ballpark. Sure! That works just fine."

A look of fear came across the face of the old black man.

Tyrone grabbed Dewey's arm. "Please sir," he pleaded quietly. "I'm not even allowed here in Canada. I'm just an ol' ballplayer trying to make a living."

Matthew tried not to look surprised. What did Tyrone mean, he wasn't allowed to be in Canada?

Dewey put down his notebook and nodded for Tyrone to continue.

"I was playing in the Negro Leagues, sir. Some of the best ball you ever will see. But then I tore my shoulder. And that was the end of ball for me. I hung around the leagues, but my playing days were over.

"One of the players with the Royals—one of the rookies

—well, he and I are friends from them days," Tyrone said. "He asked me if I wanted to come up here, with the team. I don't have no family. My shoulder was bust. So I thought this was the ticket to a new life," he concluded.

"And?" Dewey asked.

"I got me a front row seat for a little piece of history," Tyrone grinned.

"History?" The question was out before Matthew even realized what he was doing.

Tyrone turned and gave the boy a curious look. A smile danced on his face.

"Why, don't you know?" he grinned. "Negroes aren't allowed to play baseball with the white folks."

"But why?" Matthew persisted. He was too curious now to mind his manners.

Tyrone shook his head and looked at Dewey with a raised eyebrow. "Can you explain it to the boy, sir? I can't understand it neither."

Dewey sighed. "It's just the way things are in the United States. That's the way it's always been. Down South, in the southern states, black folks can't even ride the same buses as white folks. They have separate restaurants and hotels."

"Even separate washrooms!" Tyrone added.

Matthew didn't know what to say. He felt almost embarrassed looking at the old black ballplayer, wondering what it had been like for him.

"So you see, a Negro playing baseball with white folks." Tyrone whistled. "That's a piece of history."

He paused and looked down at Matthew, squinting at him with one eye.

"Say, son, did I hear you say you're a pitcher looking for a team?" Tyrone rumbled.

Matthew nodded.

"Well, I'll make you a deal." Tyrone leaned casually on his broom. "If you come here and help me out some, I'll get you into the games this summer. There's nothing like watching some big-league talent to help a pitcher grow."

Matthew stared at Tyrone, wide-eyed. He couldn't believe his luck. First, he'd found this fabulous ballpark and seen Jackie Robinson in the flesh. And now he was talking to a famous ballplayer who was going to let him come back for more!

"Were ... you ... a pitcher?" Matthew stuttered. He wanted to know everything about Tyrone's life before he came to Montreal. He noticed that Dewey, too, was listening intently.

Tyrone laughed modestly. "I played a little bit of everything."

Matthew opened his mouth to speak, the next question already on his tongue, but before he could ask, Tyrone swung his broom over his shoulder. "I'd best be moving along. Big game for Ja...." The old ballplayer stopped abruptly and turned away. "I'll see you around." The big black man shuffled off toward the tunnel next to the dugout, whistling as he went.

Dewey gathered up his camera and notebook and he and Matthew made their way to the gate. "Do you think you'll be back?" the young reporter said with a kind smile. "Sounds like it's going to be an exciting season."

"Sure thing," Matthew replied. "I'll keep an ear out here for some good leads for you."

The reporter laughed and Matthew headed off for home. He raced through the neighbourhood, which now seemed alive with colour and sound and the smell of spring sunshine. These were no longer the grey lonely streets of just a few hours ago. A trip to the ballpark had changed everything.

# Chapter Four

## *Opening Day*

### Montreal Poised for Robinson Debut

*Montreal, April 30, 1946*

By Dewey Barton

After watching Jackie Robinson's impressive road series debut from afar, Montreal fans are lining up in droves for tomorrow's home opener at Delorimier Downs.

Robinson dazzled in his road opener, with a .370 batting average, a home run, six RBIs, eight stolen bases and a whopping sixteen runs scored.

His reception has not always been cordial south of the border. But he is now on his way to a warm reception in his new hometown.

JACKIE ROBINSON'S MONTREAL DEBUT on May 1, 1946, was set to be the biggest day in the history of Delorimier Downs. The ballpark would be jammed to the rafters. Some people estimated that more than sixteen thousand raucous fans would pack the stands. Montreal, it seemed, was filled with sports fans. There was even a rumour that hockey superstar Maurice Richard would attend the game.

Since his first visit to the ballpark a few weeks ago, Matthew had been reading everything he could find about Jackie Robinson.

The Royals had opened the season with a twelve-game road trip, and Dewey's stories in the *Gazette* had kept Matthew informed of all the details. The day of the home opener, the papers were full of Jackie Robinson news.

Matthew sat at the kitchen table, reading a stack of articles he had cut from the sports sections of Alain's newspapers over the last couple of weeks. When his stepfather walked into the kitchen, he tried to hide the clippings under the placemat. The last thing he wanted to do was talk to Alain.

"What are you looking for?" Alain asked kindly as he took the milk out of the refrigerator. He lifted it at Matthew, offering him a drink, but the boy shook his head.

"Just some baseball stories," Matthew replied quietly, hoping Alain wouldn't ask anything else.

"Oh, Jackie Robinson," Alain said, sitting down at the table and picking up a paper that Matthew hadn't cut. "That's quite a story."

Matthew was surprised. He had assumed Alain wouldn't be interested in Jackie Robinson because Alain seemed to eat, drink, and sleep hockey.

"He's had quite a time, no, in the United States?" Alain nudged Matthew's clippings out from under the placemat and pointed to a picture of Robinson on the cover of the sports section from a few weeks ago. "They call him bad names and still he plays so good."

Matthew nodded. Robinson had been amazing, considering the pressure he was under. Matthew had read all about Robinson's debut in New Jersey. A crowd of more than fifty-one thousand packed the stands to be part of a turning point in baseball history. They even gave Robinson an ovation when he appeared on the field. There were jugglers and tumblers and two marching bands and the press box was crowded with reporters. Even the weather had cooperated, with clear skies and brilliant sunshine.

And Robinson hadn't disappointed. He'd had four hits, four runs batted in and two stolen bases. The crowd, reporters said, cheered and applauded the player's every move.

But the highlight of the afternoon came in his second at-bat. With two runners on and nobody out, Robinson drove the first pitch over the left-field fence for three runs. A home run! One reporter later said he heard someone in the press box swear in disbelief.

"Look at this, Matthieu." Alain pointed to a photo of George Shuba shaking hands with Jackie Robinson as he crossed home plate after his home run.

"That's one for the history books," Alain said. "A white ballplayer shaking hands with a Negro player."

"And look what he says here," Matthew added as his stepfather passed him the newspaper for a closer look. The caption under the photograph read "Handshake of the Century."

"'Shuba says he and Jackie had been together for thirty days at spring training, so he knew that Jackie was the team's best ballplayer,'" read Matthew.

"'I had no problem going to the plate to shake his hand,'" Matthew continued, reading the ballplayer's words from the newspaper.

"That's the way it should be," Alain suggested and Matthew silently agreed. His stepfather looked through a couple more newspapers, as if he was hoping the conversation would continue, but Matthew continued to read in silence.

After the historic game at Jersey City's Roosevelt Stadium—a 14–1 victory for the Royals—enthusiastic fans almost pulled the shirt off Robinson's back while he signed autographs.

But there had been tougher moments too. Matthew found the story that Billy Marsden had recounted at the ballpark, about a Syracuse player who pushed a black cat onto the field during a game and then yelled an insult at Robinson. There were even reports of other players painting their faces black. No one in the crowd ever knew, though, because the team manager wouldn't let them out on the field. At that game, Jackie went hit-less for the first time in the season.

Then, in Baltimore, the fans hurled abuse at the rookie for two straight games. The newspapers reported rumours of a fan boycott if Robinson was allowed to play. Only three thousand fans showed up for the first game of that series.

Matthew was surprised to read that Jackie wasn't the only black player in the Royals lineup in Baltimore. It seemed Branch Rickey thought it would be better to have at least two black players on the Royals, to keep Jackie company on the road trips where he often had to stay in segregated motels and restaurants away from his teammates.

John Wright was a pitcher who had joined the Royals' lineup shortly after Jackie Robinson arrived. According to the newspaper, he was also taking some abuse from the Baltimore fans. Wright came into the first game in Baltimore as a relief pitcher in the sixth inning. With the bases loaded and a five-run deficit, Wright managed to make it out of the inning without allowing a run. He completed the game, allowing no hits, although the Royals lost.

Matthew read on. For the next games in the series—a doubleheader—more than twenty-five thousand filled the stands, including an estimated ten thousand black fans. The teams split the afternoon, with one game apiece, but Jackie Robinson had a tough time. He stumbled on several fielding plays, giving some reporters cause to speculate that he was caving under pressure.

"Oh no," Matthew muttered to himself. He searched quickly for the report on the next day's game.

In the fourth game, the series finale, Robinson had three hits and scored four runs to lead the Royals to an impressive 10–0 victory.

"I don't know how he does it," Matthew said, taking a closer look at the ballplayer's face in the newspaper.

"What he is doing will change things for all his people," Alain said, eager to resume their conversation.

"But he's just a baseball player!" Matthew replied, too curious to ignore Alain any longer.

"Yes, he's a baseball player, but if he makes it to the major leagues, then he proves something about Negro people," Alain continued. "Here in Canada, we do not have the same attitude toward black people like they have in the United States. Those are feelings from deep in their history. And they will take a long time to change."

"And do you think he can make it?" Matthew asked.

"Oh, sure," said Alain. "He is a good ballplayer, or they

wouldn't have picked him. But, can he take the pressure? We will see."

His stepfather glanced at his watch. "Your mother will be late for supper tonight. Do you want me to make something for you before I go to work?"

"Oh, I'll have a sandwich," Matthew said, looking down at the newspapers to cover his confusion. "I'm going to take these to my room, if that's okay."

Alain smiled. "I will keep an eye out for more stories about your Jackie Robinson."

Matthew left the room, mumbling "thanks" under his breath.


Now, at the ballpark, Matthew's face flushed as he thought about his conversation with his stepfather. Alain tried so hard to talk to Matthew and to make him feel comfortable in Montreal. But Matthew couldn't forgive his stepfather for taking his mother away from him and the life he'd always known back in Ontario.

A deep voice startled Matthew back to reality.

"You listenin' to me, son?" Tyrone said gently. "I know it's exciting. But I have to get you sorted so I can go tend to ... well, some things that I've got to tend to."

Tyrone had been true to his word. It was opening day, and Matthew was getting ready to walk up and down the steep stairs of Delorimier Downs, selling popcorn and peanuts.

"I don't even know how to say popcorn and peanuts in French," he whispered nervously as he scrambled into the white shirt and blue pants that Tyrone had pulled out of a cupboard, in the locker room below the grandstand. He carefully placed on his head the white cap that all park vendors were required to wear. The others were already heading out to their positions around the stadium. There were two dozen or so roving vendors and each one had a separate territory, marked on a map that hung in the locker room. Matthew glanced nervously at the unfamiliar names: Justine, Nicolas, Leonce, Daniel. They had all ignored Matthew and Tyrone. The teens spent most of their time snapping back and forth in French, so fast that Matthew couldn't understand a word they said. But he got the sense they weren't too happy to see him there.

"It don't matter that you don't know no French," Tyrone told him with a grin. "If they want peanuts or popcorn, you'll know about it. And besides, I've got you someone to show you the ropes."

Tyrone opened the door. A boy, about Matthew's age, was standing outside, looking around nervously. Matthew had seen him in the locker room earlier, but he had changed quietly in a corner, away from the noisy group.

"*Vite*, Monsieur Tyrone," the boy said. He gave Matthew a quick look and nodded his approval. "*C'est bon.*"

"He'll do, will he, René?" Tyrone smiled. "You keep an eye on him, you understand?"

The boy nodded. He was about the same height as Matthew but had dark hair and dark eyes. He was slight and had pulled his belt as tight as it could go in order to keep the blue pants from falling down.

"Aren't you supposed to be in school?" Matthew asked.

"It's a day *historique*," the boy replied, flashing a friendly smile that lightened up his otherwise serious face. "All the children of the neighbourhood get the day off school. This is a *vacance*, a holiday for all. To celebrate Jackie Robinson." René paused, giving Matthew a curious look from behind the dark bangs that hung over his forehead. "Why aren't you in school?"

"Um, I finished the year already," Matthew mumbled. "In Pembroke, where I live. I mean, where I used to live."

Just then, Tyrone pushed them out the door and pointed to a tray of popcorn and peanuts. "Time to go, boys."

"This way," said René as he headed to one of the gates. In the distance, the boys could hear the roar of the crowd as the Royals were introduced.

"My name is René Deslauriers," the boy said as they walked toward the stands. René flashed another grin.

"I'm Matthew Parker." Matthew smiled back gratefully. Then, he took a deep breath and followed René out into the ballpark.

The grass glistened under the late afternoon sun and the ballpark was filled with the sights, sounds, and smells of the game. All eyes, however, were fixed on second base, where Jackie Robinson was tossing a ball back and forth with Al Campanis.

"This is history," Matthew muttered joyfully to himself. He had a brief pang of guilt as he smiled over at René. This was the kind of moment he'd always wanted to share with A.J. But right then, Pembroke seemed very, very far away.

For the rest of the afternoon, Matthew divided his attention between the excitement on the field and his new job. He followed René's example, walking up and down the aisles, stopping whenever someone in the crowd waved him down. Peanuts and popcorn were ten cents a bag. Some of the older boys carried hot dogs, coffee, and bottled soda. At the start of the game, all of the vendors were given a stack of scorecards to sell at a price of a nickel apiece. Although the spectators kept him busy, Matthew always made sure he was up at the top of the stairs and out of the range of customers whenever Jackie Robinson came up to the plate.

The Royals had an impressive lineup around Robinson and several other players quickly became fan favourites. Some were Dodger veterans, like pitcher Curt

Davis and catcher Herman Franks. There were also players, like Jackie, hoping to make the jump to the big-league Brooklyn team, including Marvin "Rabbit" Rackley and Tom Tatum.

But this day was about Jackie Robinson. The crowd cheered wildly no matter what he did. They even applauded pop-ups. Later, even Jackie admitted it wasn't his best game, and certainly not the way he wanted to greet his new fans. Unfortunately, his only hit came late, when the Royals were already trailing 13–8.

As soon as Robinson was on base, the crowd began to chant, "*Allez, allez!*" They wanted a stolen base. From his position in the stands, Matthew figured the chances were good. Robinson was great at taking bases. Once, he'd so flustered an opposing pitcher with his moves on and off the base that the pitcher had completely misfired the ball. Robinson ended up stealing home, all the way from first.

Matthew held his breath every time Robinson inched his way off the base. For someone so big and muscular, Jackie's feet moved like a dancer's. But his teammate grounded out, and the inning ended before Robinson got a chance to strut his stuff for the hometown fans.

"He'll do better next time," Tyrone chuckled as he came up beside Matthew. "You ain't seen nothing yet, son. He learned plenty of those moves on the football field," the old man added. "He was a star football player, too. At a big university in California."

Tyrone scanned the opening day crowd with a look of delight on his face. "I never thought I'd see this day," he said, shaking his head. "Jackie didn't neither."

"You know Jackie Robinson?" Matthew asked eagerly.

"Back to work, boy." Tyrone gave him a gentle tap on the shoulder. "That's a story for another day. These folks want their peanuts and popcorn now."

The Royals lost the home opener, 13–9, but none of the fans left unhappy. After the last pitch, Robinson was swarmed on the field, surrounded by men, women, and children in search of autographs. The hearty reaction the crowd had given the Royals rookie made Matthew feel sort of proud. It was certainly different from the stories he'd read in the American newspapers. Reluctantly, Matthew and René went to turn in their uniforms and money to the park manager.

"She wants to know if you can work all summer," René muttered, translating what the large, dark-haired woman behind the counter was saying in rapid-fire French. She gave him a smile.

"*Oui*," Matthew nodded back, sending René into peals of laughter. He tugged at Matthew's shirt sleeve.

"Let's get out of here before she realizes you don't speak French," he laughed.

"I do speak French," Matthew said, pretending to sound offended. "*Les arachides* are peanuts and *maïs soufflé* is popcorn. That's all I need to know!"

The boys laughed as they made their way back to the stands. Jackie Robinson was still on the field, signing autographs. They settled into a pair of seats behind home plate, watching the scene below.

"The others won't be very happy," René said, his face turning serious.

"The others?" Matthew asked.

René shrugged. "The other boys and girls, they are, how you say? Trouble."

"Trouble?" Matthew repeated back. "Why?"

René sighed. "They want all the customers and all the money for themselves. *Bien oui,* they can't be every-where in the stadium. But they like to keep out newcomers. Like me. And you. Just be careful," René said. Then he pointed at the field.

One of the coaches was carefully leading Robinson through the crowd of admirers, but the rookie player seemed reluctant to pass by anyone who asked for an autograph.

"See over there?" René pointed to a small group of onlookers a few sections away. "That's Madame Robinson. Her name is Rachel."

Matthew looked over at a youngish black woman, her eyes pinned on the player at the centre of the crowd. Another black woman and a black man, with a camera and notebook, stood with her.

"How do you know Mrs. Robinson?" Matthew asked.

"They live in my neighbourhood," René explained. "In a place on de Gaspé. They are the talk of the street."

"Where is that? I haven't lived here very long,"

René gave him a sympathetic smile. "*Oui*, it's a big city when you first arrive, *je sais*. Where we live, rue de Gaspé, it's where lots of the working people live," he continued. "You know, lots of *appartements*. I must take two streetcars and a bus to get here, *comprends*?

"And so do Monsieur and Madame Robinson," René added. "My friends have seen them on the streetcar from the boarding house. Just like me!"

"A boarding house? I'd have thought they could afford something fancier than that," Matthew replied. Immediately, he wished he could take his words back. The last thing he wanted was to hurt his new friend's feelings. "I mean, I pictured them at the Ritz Carlton, or one of those other posh hotels downtown."

René frowned. "I don't know if Jackie Robinson could even stay at that hotel. You know, because he's coloured."

"Even Jackie Robinson?" Matthew was amazed.

"My mother says Madame Robinson was worried she wouldn't find a place to stay at all, anywhere in Montreal. That's what she told the lady she boards with, Madame Cousineau. Maman plays cards with madame, so she got the whole story.

"Madame Cousineau, she makes Madame Robinson

use all her linen and her dishes. And madame, she is very kind to everyone in the building. Even though she speaks no French, she leaves her door open and has a bowl of fruit that all the children can come and take from.

"Madame Cousineau says madame and Jackie will have a baby in this winter," René said shyly. "It will be a very lucky baby to have so famous a father."

The two boys looked over again at Rachel Robinson, who had not taken her eyes off her husband. "And that man with her? He's a reporter with an American newspaper, and a friend to the Robinsons."

Matthew and René watched as Jackie Robinson was finally escorted off the field.

"Well, that was quite a day," said René, as he watched the crowd disperse. He stood to leave as well. "So I'll see you next game, *bon*?"

Matthew smiled shyly. "*Merci*, René, *pour tout*. Thanks for everything."

"So, you do speak French!" René laughed as he disappeared down the tunnel that led to the gate.

Matthew took one last look at the ball diamond, now turning red and orange in the setting sun.

"See you, Jackie," he whispered. "You did it."

## Chapter Five

# *Lessons from the Past*

**Partlow Struggles in Debut**
by Dewey Barton
*Montreal, June 6, 1946*
The second Negro player in the Royals' lineup has failed to follow in the footsteps of his speedy counterpart from second base.

Roy Partlow, the Negro southpaw for the Royals, was pounded in the fifth inning of his organized baseball debut. Syracuse scored three runs before Partlow was yanked. The Chiefs went on to a 6–5 victory, taking the series three games to two.

Meanwhile, league-leading hitter Jackie Robinson remains sidelined for a seventh straight game.

AS SPRING WARMED toward summer, Delorimier Downs became like a second home to Matthew. It was a massive building, right in the heart of Montreal's east end. Home plate was at the corner of Ontario and Delorimier streets, with Delorimier running along the third base line. There was Lariviere Street on one side, Parthenais Street on the other. Matthew now knew the exact moment when he would turn the corner and see the Knit-to-Fit building and its water tower. He sometimes wondered how they ever jammed such a big stadium into such a tiny space.

As he walked to and from the ballpark each day, Matthew had lots of time to think. More and more these days, he was thinking about Jackie Robinson and the Montreal Royals, and not about his life back in Pembroke, although he still missed A.J. a great deal.

A.J. Kirkpatrick was Matthew's best friend. He lived just down the street from the Parker house and the two boys had spent every summer together since they were toddlers. A.J. was tall and scrawny, with a wild head of red hair and lots of freckles. Matthew was a few inches shorter, but could outrun his friend every time. Matthew's hair turned blond in the summer sunshine, and he, too, sported a face full of freckles. He loved sports, and was always running or jumping or throwing something.

Still, maybe because he'd had no dad around, Matthew was often quieter than his best friend. He spent a lot of his time at home, quietly reading books, or helping his grandmother in the kitchen, or his granddad in the yard.

"You act like a grown-up," A.J. often teased. "And stop

taking school so serious. Can't you lighten up for a change?"

When Matthew told him the news about moving to Montreal, A.J. just shook his head. They were playing catch in the schoolyard around the corner, just as they had every spring. The air was sweet with the aroma of freshly cut grass and the music of songbirds filled the country air. But best of all was the feel of their baseball gloves, which never left their sides. The boys had spent the winter working in linseed oil to give them that special supple feel. To Matthew and A.J., linseed oil on leather was the best spring smell of all!

"All they do is play hockey there," A.J. said knowingly. "And they don't speak a word of English."

He paused as he caught the ball and hurled it back to his friend. The two lived and breathed baseball every summer and were the best pitcher and catcher team in their age group.

"But I don't play hockey and I don't speak French," Matthew replied.

"When do you go?"

"Next weekend."

"Next weekend!" A.J. gasped. Matthew nodded. It was too soon.

"What about the baseball season? We don't have another pitcher."

Matthew just shrugged. The boys tossed the ball back

and forth in silence. A few days later, Matthew was gone.

Since then, Matthew had written several letters to A.J., trying to share the excitement of seeing Jackie Robinson and the Montreal Royals. His mother was helping him with his latest letter and he read aloud what he had carefully printed so far.

"'Jackie Robinson got hit in the wrist. Some say the pitcher did it on purpose. The next game, he had a double and stole a base. He sure showed them. I wish you could be here to see him play! Tyrone says someday I may even get to meet Jackie!'"

"Matthew, dear, your letter is all about Jackie Robinson!" his mother exclaimed. "Isn't there anything else you want to tell your friend?"

"There's more," Matthew said. "I ask him how our team is doing, too: 'Hope you're doing okay with Timmy Riley pitching,'" Matthew continued. "'I wish I could be there. But I wish you could be here, too.'"

Matthew paused, his face reddening slightly as he felt his mother's eyes on him.

"Does this mean you're starting to like Montreal?" she asked in a gentle voice.

Matthew folded the letter, readying it for its envelope. He was confused. He loved the time he spent at Delorimier Downs. But writing this letter to A.J. brought back memories of home.

"I don't know, Mom, I really don't know," Matthew said. He got up abruptly and headed to his room.

More than a month had passed since the season opener, and Matthew had been at the ballpark almost every day. It had taken some convincing, but Alain had helped smooth things over with his mother.

"It's a great chance for him," Alain said. "How many boys get to spend the summer at a big-league ballpark? He is learning some French—and some baseball—all at the same time." Alain smiled at Matthew, who looked away.

"Maybe Alain could come down to the ballpark with you sometime and check it out?" his mother suggested.

Matthew gave her a cold look. His mother flushed with irritation.

"Maybe we'll all go down there together one day," she concluded in a pointed voice. But they never had.

It was early June and getting warmer every day. Tyrone had put in a good word for Matthew with the grounds crew supervisor, and Matthew was often allowed to help out with clean up. Hardly any of the vendors were around between games, but everyone seemed to accept Matthew's presence as normal. He was beyond grateful to Tyrone. It often felt crowded at the apartment with his mother and Alain. It was as if he was an intruder on their time together; that they'd be happier alone. So he made a point of spending as much time as he could away from home. He only wished René was around more. The only time he saw his new friend was when the Royals were in town.

But Matthew did get to see a lot of Dewey Barton. The cub reporter made a point of looking for Matthew whenever he was down at the ballpark, sniffing around for stories.

"Any sign of Jackie?" Matthew heard Dewey's voice behind him and looked up from the stack of programs he was sorting. He shook his head.

"I want to find out more about this calf injury of his," Dewey mused, tapping his pencil on his notebook.

"He sure has been playing well!" Matthew enthused.

"Yes, he has," Dewey said, flipping pages. "A triple, a pair of singles, two runs, and stolen base against Buffalo. He's batting .356. But now he's hurt."

"I hope he's going to be okay," Matthew said. "Lots of folks come out to the ballpark just to see him play. And the Royals are in first place!"

"Well, the team's on the road now for twenty games," Dewey replied. "I'm heading out to meet them in Baltimore in a couple of days. That's where Jackie has trouble. Those fans are some of the worst in the league."

Matthew frowned, worried for the player and the team.

"Hey kid, don't worry," Dewey said, giving him a playful punch in the shoulder. "Branch Rickey's not going to let anything happen to Jackie Robinson. How's your arm coming along?"

Matthew shook his head. "I don't get to play any more. No one around here plays ball. They all play hockey."

Dewey gave him an understanding smile. "I know what you mean. What else do you miss?"

"Well, if I was home right now, I'd be down at the fishing pond with A.J. and the rest of the boys," Matthew said. The reporter nodded for the boy to continue. "My grandpa and A.J. taught me stuff like that. You know. Fishing. Baseball."

He had an envelope full of photographs of Colin MacLean, but neither his mother nor his grandparents talked much about him. When Matthew was born, he was given the name Parker—his mother's last name— rather than his father's. His mother said it was just less confusing. His father's parents had died years ago. Matthew had only vague memories of them and his only uncle, who was killed in France during the war.

Matthew had never known any home other than the red brick house that he and his mother shared with her parents. So it had been a huge shock when Grace told Matthew that she was marrying Alain and they were moving to Montreal. Matthew begged her to let him stay in Pembroke with his grandparents.

"This is home," Matthew had argued, trying to hold back his tears. He was not going to cry in front of his mother. He had to stay calm so he could make her change her mind. "Why can't we stay here?"

"Because Alain is from Montreal and has a chance for a job there," she'd replied. "Granny and Grandpa are getting old. And besides, you and Alain and I are going to be a family now," Grace explained. "You'll have all sorts of new experiences in Montreal. We'll get to learn French and you'll get to live in a big city," his mother said encouragingly.

"I don't want to learn French and I don't want to live in a big city," Matthew retorted. "And I don't want to be a family. So, you two go. I'd just be in the way."

His mother looked so hurt that Matthew had regretted his words. He and his mother never used to argue like this. Until she met Alain, he'd had her all to himself. First, Alain had taken away his mother, and now, the only home he'd ever known.

"Do you really mean that?" his mother had asked, tears now welling up in her eyes.

"I guess not. I mean, no," Matthew had stammered. "I don't know what I mean."

The possibility of Matthew staying in Pembroke had never come up again.

"That's tough, kid," Dewey's voice brought Matthew back to the present. Matthew gave him a grateful smile. He hadn't really told anyone how he had ended up in Montreal.

"You know, things are going to work out," Dewey added. "They're going to work out for you. And for Jackie Robinson. But right now, I've got to go!" He jumped up as he saw one of the Royals managers heading toward the gate. "Hang in there, Matt."

With Dewey gone, Matthew finished sorting his programs and decided to take a break. He hopped the low fence that ran around the field and made his way onto the grass. It was soft under his feet and perfectly green, the white lines absolutely straight and the bases spotless. He paused and looked around the stadium. It looked enormous. The top sections were covered by an overhanging roof, but the lower part of the stands was wide open, subject to the whims of Mother Nature. The far seats in the outfield were also open to the elements. The walls around the stadium weren't very high and kids in the neighbourhood often spent games patrolling up and down the sidewalks. If they got a foul ball, they could return it at the front gate and get free admission for the rest of the game.

Looking up at the massive grandstand, Matthew tried to imagine what they would look like jammed with screaming fans, the way they had been since Robinson came to town.

Matthew gazed down the field at the back wall and the scoreboard. He stood at home plate and set his feet, pretending he was holding a bat. He swung—and away it went! In his mind at least.

"That's a long ways away," he muttered.

"That's some swing."

Matthew turned to see Tyrone, leaning on his rake and laughing to himself.

"You remind me of Cool Papa Bell."

"Who?"

Tyrone shook his head. "I should've known as much. You've never heard of the greats of the Negro Leagues, have you?"

"Sorry," Matthew said, shaking his head. "But I am learning a lot about hockey."

Tyrone laughed. "How did I end up in this crazy country? All you folks talk about is hockey. Even in the heat of the summer when I'd just as soon forget about the ice and the cold."

"Who was Cool Papa Bell?" Matthew persisted. He'd always thought the old man had a story to tell. Maybe this would be his chance to hear it.

Tyrone looked around. None of the grounds crew was around.

The old ballplayer motioned for Matthew to follow him down into the dugout. Tyrone sat down in Jackie Robinson's usual spot. Matthew eagerly sat down close by.

It was the first time Matthew had been in the dugout and he soaked in the smell of chewing tobacco and liniment and sweat. This was where the Royals watched the game. This was as close as he might ever get to being a real ballplayer.

"The Negro Leagues, that's some of the best baseball you'll ever see," Tyrone began. "You see, we black people can't play in the big leagues. At least not yet." He smiled and pointed up to Jackie Robinson's picture on an old newspaper in the dugout. "So, in the 1920s, a fella decided to give us our own league. We'd travel around, mainly to places with lots of black fans. And we'd dazzle them." Tyrone grinned at the memory.

"You'd see plays you'll never see in no major league ballpark. We were the fastest, could jump the highest, and hit the hardest. And we put on a pretty good show.

"There were some great ballplayers in those days: Satchel Paige, Josh Gibson, Buck Leonard, Hilton Smith, and Cool Papa Bell. When I watch Jackie run bases, I know he learned that from Cool Papa. You'd look at him one minute, two or three steps off the base. The next minute, he was gone."

"And you?"

Tyrone chuckled. "I wasn't too bad. I played hard and I was a smart ballplayer. But I was no Satchel Paige."

The old man paused and stared out at the field, as if he could still picture it in his mind.

"Satchel could do it all. He was a lean, mean baseball machine. He could pitch. He could play any position you put him at. And he could hit like there was no tomorrow."

"So why didn't Satchel make it to the big leagues?" Matthew asked, mesmerized.

Tyrone shook his head sadly and pointed to his arm. "Nothing but the colour of his skin, boy. Nothing but the colour of his skin kept Satchel from making baseball history."

"Well, what about Jackie Robinson?" Matthew was confused. "If Satchel was so good, why wasn't he the one?"

"It's all about timing," Tyrone explained. "Satchel was good in his day but the world wasn't ready for a Negro ballplayer—especially not one as good as Satchel. Mr. Rickey, he looked long and hard before he picked Jackie Robinson. He had to find the right person or his experiment was not going to work.

"And it takes a special person to do what Jackie's doing," he continued. "Not everyone could take the heat he's taking. Imagine folks calling you names and throwing things at you and threatening your life. And all you want to do is play ball."

Matthew knew a lot about what was happening to Jackie Robinson, but he'd never heard about the threats on his life. He was shocked.

"But it's just a game. Why would they say stuff like that?"

"But it's not just a game, my young friend. If we black folks get to play baseball, then what's next? Are we goin' to want to come into your restaurants and ride your buses and stay in your fancy hotels?

"Why, not even Mr. Hopper wanted Jackie," Tyrone continued. Matthew looked at the old ballplayer with surprise. Clay Hopper always seemed eager to tell the reporters how well Jackie Robinson was doing. Why wouldn't he have wanted Jackie?

As if reading his mind, Tyrone went on. "Clay, he comes from the South. He owns a cotton plantation there. So, he had no intention of being the first manager with a Negro on his team. That would be a disgrace to his family and friends. Matter of fact, he begged Mr. Rickey not to make him do it."

"But he did!" Matthew exclaimed.

The old ballplayer shrugged as he got up slowly and picked up his rake. "Mr. Hopper likes to win just as much as the next man."

That reminded Matthew of a big story in *Newsweek* magazine about Jackie Robinson. It had quoted the Royals manager singing the praises of his star second baseman: "He's a player who must go to the majors," Hopper had said. "He's a big-league ballplayer, a good team hustler, and a real gentleman."

"Yep, you just remember Satchel Paige," Tyrone said, breaking into Matthew's thoughts. He started to walk away with his rake, then paused.

"By the way, boy, why aren't you in school? I see you

down here all the time." Tyrone gave Matthew a suspicious look.

"I just moved here," Matthew explained. "From Ontario. And the school year's almost over. So my mom and Alain said I could just have the summer off.

"And," he added sheepishly, "I don't really know anybody. So I'm not too excited about going to school."

"But you are going back to school?" Tyrone said, his eyes narrowing.

Matthew laughed. "I'm only twelve! Of course, I'm going back to school. I'm even going to learn French. Though I'm not sure my mom would be too happy about some of the words I'm learning down here."

Tyrone gave a hearty laugh. "Glad to hear it, boy. Baseball's great, but your schooling comes first. Jackie Robinson's a college graduate. That's another reason why he's here."

Matthew wanted to know more—and he sensed that Tyrone had more to tell—but just then, the grounds crew appeared. Denis, the supervisor, waved over to Tyrone and Matthew.

"*Eh, vous!* You playing ball or working?" He grinned at the two of them. "*Et toi*, Tyrone. You may have famous friends but you're stuck with us for now. Let's do some work, *oui?*"

Tyrone shuffled up the steps to the ball field. He playfully waved his ball cap at the empty stands, the way players did after a home run. "*Merci, merci.*"

Everyone laughed as they got to work. Matthew picked up a rake to help. As he gently raked the smooth dirt of the infield, he thought about what Denis had said. Who were Tyrone's famous friends? Did he mean Satchel Paige and the players from the old days? And why did Tyrone always talk about Jackie Robinson as if he had known him somewhere before he came to Montreal?

That night, at supper, Matthew told his mother and Alain more about Tyrone.

"He sounds like quite a character," his mother smiled.

"Tyrone's always talking about how black people can't go into certain restaurants or on buses or in some hotels. It's weird." Matthew said.

He saw his mother and Alain exchange a look.

"I know. It's hard to explain," his mother started. "Because it's not like that here in Canada. It's called segregation. And it's not everywhere in the United States either, just some parts."

"So they're really not allowed to go some places?"

"I heard all about it during the war," Alain jumped in. "The black soldiers from the States had to fight, same as the white ones. But when they went back home, they'd have to sit in a different part of the bus. And they'd have a separate part of the restaurant for coloured people.

Even separate schools."

"But why?" Matthew persisted.

Alain shrugged. "That's how they treat the Negroes in the South. For a long time, these people were slaves. And I guess some Americans have never learned to treat them fairly."

"So Jackie Robinson is a big deal? Playing for the Royals?"

"Sure," said Alain. "They don't always want to be treated like that, *non?* Every time one of them breaks through into some place they weren't allowed before, they are all that much closer."

"Even a sport?"

"Even a sport," his mother replied. "That's why they call it 'breaking the colour barrier.' He's proving he can play with the white players."

All at once, a frown came across her face. "Alain, do you think Matt is safe at the ballpark? I mean, with all this fuss over Jackie Robinson? It sounds as if things are quite ugly at some of the ballparks where he goes."

"*Bien sur*," Alain replied. "The people of Montreal are taking very good care of Mr. Jackie Robinson. In the newspaper, they say people ask for his autograph everywhere he goes. He's almost as popular as *les Canadiens*."

"He's even going to be an umpire at a softball game with the Canadiens!" Matthew said.

"Okay, okay," his mother smiled. "He sounds wonderful."

Later that night, Matthew thought about what his mom and Alain had said. Was Jackie Robinson really about more than baseball?

## Chapter Six

# *Taking the Heat*

### Orioles Flap Their Wings at Royals' Robinson
by Dewey Barton
*Baltimore, June 19, 1946*

The Royals' road trip seems to be taking its toll. Earlier this month, the Orioles continued their efforts to ground the high-flying Jackie Robinson. Robinson exchanged words with Orioles first baseman Eddie Robinson. The Negro player accused the Oriole of kicking him in the back on a double play. The Baltimore player claimed the blow was accidental.

These kinds of accidents appear to be affecting Robinson. He played two games in May with a bandaged left hand. Now he is out with a "mysterious ailment" afflicting his thigh. The leg has been described to this reporter as "blue as well as black."

MATTHEW TOOK OFF HIS BALL CAP and wiped his brow. His hair was even blonder than usual and he had sprouted a face full of new freckles thanks to all the time he was spending outdoors. It was the middle of June and his mother kept teasing him that he was growing faster than the weeds in the vacant lot up the street. It was true—he'd already had to move up a size in the ballpark uniforms because the pants and shirt were both suddenly too short.

It was a steamy summer day in Montreal; much hotter and more humid than Matthew ever remembered it being in Pembroke. In the neighbourhoods around the ballpark, older couples sat out on their balconies, trying to keep cool. The men stripped down to their undershirts and the women fanned themselves. Many families hauled buckets of water out to the street so the children could splash one another. The lucky ones got to play in a fountain of water from the local fire hydrant.

The crew at Delorimier Downs had been out working in the noonday sun, preparing the field for an afternoon game. Matthew settled into a seat in a shady section of the stadium. He munched happily on a hot dog as he read the program for the upcoming game. He frowned as he looked at the roster for the Royals. Would Jackie Robinson play today?

"Hey kid, can I grab a peek at that program?"

"Sure, Dewey."

Matthew hadn't seen Dewey for a while. He had been on the road with the Royals.

"I hear rumours that Robinson's out again," Matthew said, trying to hide his disappointment.

"Yep, that's what I'm hearing, too," said Dewey.

"We won't know for sure until they announce the lineup. But I betcha there's going to be some disappointed fans this afternoon," he added, taking off his hat and laying it on the seat next to him. He rolled up his sleeves to try to cool off in the sweltering midday heat.

"To tell you the truth, I'm not sure what's wrong," he said thoughtfully.

"What do you mean? The team is saying it's a pulled muscle."

Dewey shrugged his shoulders. "That's what they're saying. A severe calf strain. But I've wondered since the start if that was really what was bothering him."

"He went on the road trip, didn't he?" Matthew said. He added in a shy voice, "I was reading your stories from the trip."

"I guess they wanted him to stay with the team. Keep his head in the game," Dewey explained. "It sure was something to see. Something I wish I never did see, to tell you the truth."

"I saw the pictures you took in Baltimore."

"It was scary. All those fans out on the field. And then they surrounded the clubhouse, calling Jackie all kinds of names. Saying, 'We know you're in there. We're gonna get you.'" Dewey shook his head. "I don't get it.

He's just another player. But down there, they just can't see it."

"So when's he going to play again?"

"No one knows," Dewey replied. "At least the Royals are winning. Or things would be even worse for Jackie."

"What's that new pitcher like?" Matthew asked, consulting the program for his name. "Roy Partlow."

Dewey grinned. "Oh, you mean the other black player on the team? Isn't that the darnedest thing? Everyone is all over Jackie Robinson, but the Royals have had two other black players."

"That other fella didn't stay very long, did he?" Matthew puzzled.

"Who's your friend, Dewey?"

Matthew looked up to see Sam Hill, the reporter from the United States. He had seen Hill many times around the ballpark. His wife often sat with Rachel Robinson, while he joined the rest of the reporters.

"Why don't you join us, Sam? I'll go get us a couple of dogs," Dewey said with a smile. "This is Matthew. He just moved here from Ontario, same as me. He's working the summer at the ballpark—a real fan of the game."

"Pleased to meet you, Matthew." The young black reporter leaned over and shook hands.

"We were just talking about John Wright and Roy Partlow," Dewey explained.

Sam shook his head. "I felt badly for John. And I'm

not sure things are going to be much better for Roy."

"What do you mean?" Dewey asked.

"The Royals didn't want Jackie to be the only black face on the team. So they brought up John to keep him company. Maybe take some of the heat off Jackie. When they were at training camp in Florida, they lived together, away from the team. John had been in the military, too. And he was from the South, from New Orleans. So the Royals thought he'd be tough enough to handle what was coming.

"John even played in Baltimore, that first trip. The bases were loaded when he came in. It was the sixth inning, Royals down by five. He held them in the sixth and finished the game. Didn't give up a hit."

As Hill spoke, it was as if he was replaying the game in his head. Matthew wondered what it was like for him, watching what was happening to the black players.

"But John didn't get to play much after that," Sam continued. "No one really knows why. But after he left, Jackie told me that John couldn't handle it—the abusive fans; the pressure of being one of the first; the constant speculation of whether he would make it to the big leagues or fail. It was all too much for him.

"So now they've brought in Roy, from the Negro Leagues. He's a lefty with some big-time experience. Trouble is he says he's thirty, but I'd say he's thirty-five, maybe even thirty-six. That arm isn't what it used to be."

Sam shook his head. "I just hope he can stick it out. Not that it makes much difference to the way those rednecks treat Jackie. But at least he's not the only one."

Matthew soaked in everything the American reporter was saying. Dewey had told him that Sam Hill was actually close friends with the Robinsons. He had been a stringer for a few years, mainly covering sports. But now, he'd been hired by a black newspaper called the *Pittsburgh Courier* to follow Jackie Robinson through his rookie season. Matthew asked how it felt to be given such an important job.

"I guess they figure because I met Jackie in the army, I can give them some kind of coverage they might not otherwise get," Sam said with a chuckle. "Hey, if this is my big break, that's okay, too. Jackie gets a kick out of it. He says I'm just riding his shirttails. And I tell him I'm holding on tight because it's probably going to be a bumpy ride."

"How's the calf strain?" Dewey asked Sam, as he returned with the hot dogs.

Hill turned to Matthew and gave him a playful wink. "Don't ask me that, Dewey! You know there are some things I just can't tell you. Rachel's starting to mind the heat though. I guess it's tough being pregnant in the summer. And she worries about Jackie. Especially when he's away on the road.

"They take good care of her in the neighbourhood,"

Sam continued. "All the ladies bring over food and check on her if they don't see her. And my wife, she tries to keep an eye on Rachel as much as she can."

Sam looked around to see if anyone was listening. Matthew moved in a bit closer to make sure he wouldn't miss whatever nugget the American reporter was about to share.

"Dewey, you didn't hear it from me, but Jackie's been keeping some pretty good company the last couple of days," Hill said in a soft voice. "He's been down at Joe Louis's training camp in New Jersey. Joe's getting ready for the big title fight against Billy Conn."

"Wow!" Dewey exclaimed. "And you can't report that either!"

Matthew gave a little gasp at the mention of Joe Louis. The "Brown Bomber," as he was called in the newspapers, was the heavyweight champion of the world! And now he was friends with Jackie Robinson!

Sam shook his head. "Jack made me promise not to tell. But you can see he's moving up in the world."

"I'll say! Joe Louis is big news these days!" Dewey whistled.

"I guess the two of them have plenty to talk about," Sam suggested. "The rest of us can only imagine what Jack's going through. I mean, I get pushed around every once in a while when we go South. And I get stuck in the same rattraps as him most times while the white reporters get the fancy hotel rooms. But I get some protection because I can hide behind my camera and notebook," Hill added. "That's a far cry from being out on a baseball field in front of tens of thousands of screaming fans."

A voice came over the loudspeaker. "*Mesdames et messieurs, bienvenue à Delorimier Downs.* Ladies and gentlemen, welcome to Delorimier Downs. Okay, sounds good. *Ça va bien.*"

"I guess it's time to get back to work," Sam sighed, getting up from his chair and picking up his camera and notebook.

"See you later, Matthew," Sam said as he turned to go. "Pleasure to meet you."

"You too, sir," Matthew replied politely.

It had been a pleasure. Matthew liked Sam Hill. And now he felt like he understood a little better what life was like for Jackie Robinson and the other black players.

"It's almost hard to believe, isn't it?" Dewey said, watching the other reporter walk up the stairs toward the press box.

"He has to work so much harder at everything he does," Dewey continued. "Just because his skin is a different colour from mine. Even though we're both reporters. And to make it even tougher, he has to balance his friendship with Jackie with being a good reporter."

Matthew nodded. "It seems so unfair. I just don't get it, Dewey."

"There's nothing to get, Matt," Dewey said, gathering his jacket and hat to head up to the press box. "There is nothing to get. It's plain wrong. But it's just going to take some people a little longer to figure that out. That's what Jackie Robinson's all about."

And then he frowned. "That is, if he'd ever make it back into the lineup. Wish me luck, kid. I've got to find out what's really going on."

After splitting an earlier doubleheader with one win each, the Royals managed to close out the Syracuse series with a win, even with Robinson out of the lineup. And the star player's absence gave fans a chance to cheer for some of the other Royals. Branch Rickey had made certain that the team had plenty of talent. Quebec-born player Jean Pierre Roy was a favourite with the fans, as was the speedy Rabbit Rackley.

Jackie Robinson had made a name for himself as a daring base stealer, but Marvin Rackley actually led the league in stolen bases. Some reporters said it was a toss-up as to who was faster: Robinson or Rackley.

The Royals were trailing Syracuse 2–1 in the sixth when catcher Dixie Howell started a rally with a double. He later came in to score the tying run on Marvin Rackley's single. The Syracuse players were instantly on edge.

Later in the inning, with the bases loaded, George

Shuba hit a shallow ball to centre field. The Syracuse second baseman caught the ball in an awkward position, with his back to home plate. And that was all the opening Rabbit Rackley needed. He was off for home plate to score what would be the winning run.

"What a play!" Matthew yelled to René, who was trying not to spill his peanuts and popcorn as he cheered Rackley's daring dash.

"That's why they call him *le Lapin*—'the Rabbit'!" René grinned back.

The Royals took the game with a final score of 4–2 and the fans left the ballpark in good humour. Their team was back in first place, even without Jackie Robinson.

As Matthew joined the other vendors in the post-game clean up, he was startled to hear shouting coming from one section of the stands. He looked over to see René shoving another boy. He moved closer but René caught his eye and gave a shake of his head. Matthew backed off, but stayed close enough to hear what the two were arguing about.

"*Maudit anglais,*" yelled the other boy, turning and spitting in Matthew's direction, "*Et maudit negres. Et toi, maudit indien.*"

Startled, Matthew ducked back behind the stands. He remembered now René's earlier warning—to stay away from the other vendors. René had told him that most of the teenagers had dropped out of school and spent their time roving the streets of the east end. Some had even been in trouble with the police, but Cecile had a soft spot for them, having grown up in the east end herself. René said she had a hard time firing the hooligans, no matter how bad they got. Seeing the boys picking on his friend, Matthew was worried. But he didn't know where to go for help.

A few minutes later, René appeared. The boy's face was red and sweaty and a bruise was starting to form on one of his cheeks.

"What happened?" Matthew gasped.

René shook his head. "*Ça ne fait rien.* It doesn't matter."

"No," Matthew persisted. "It does matter! Why was he spitting at me? What did I do wrong? And what was that other word he used?"

René sighed. "It's not what you did wrong. It's just his brother—he was kicked off the job here. And now François, he blames you. But really, it was Tyrone who turned him in. He saw Pierre stealing money from one of the cash boxes."

"But I didn't do anything to him."

"Oui," René agreed. "But you are *anglais* and so it is easy for François to blame you. I will tell Tyrone to watch out for him. You should, too. Stay away from him. He is bad business."

René went back to sweeping up the debris and Matthew did the same. He was still surprised by the other boy's anger toward him. Just because he was English? It didn't make any sense.

"Another win," said René, changing the subject. "They're starting to win as much as *les Canadiens!*"

"I think the Royals will win the pennant for sure," Matthew said, smiling at his friend's reference to hockey. "That would be a perfect finish to Jackie Robinson's first season."

"You think he's going to last that long?" René frowned. "The boys on the crew are betting he won't be back."

"Not be back? Why?"

"They say there's nothing wrong with his leg. They say he just can't take the pressure. He's ready to crack." René waved his hand around the side of his head in the "cuckoo" sign.

"Do you believe that?" Matthew said anxiously.

His friend shrugged. "I don't know what to believe. He seems so calm and quiet when he's here. But then you hear the stories about what happens at the other ball fields. Who knows? It could be true."

Matthew hoped it wasn't. He was pulling for Jackie Robinson.

## Chapter Seven

# *Jackie Makes a Comeback*

### Robinson Struggles to Stay in Royals' Lineup

by Dewey Barton

*June 23, 1946*

Jackie Robinson has been in and out of the Royals' lineup in June, much to the frustration of the Montreal fans.

Robinson finally made his comeback in Friday night's twin-bill opener against the Newark Bears. But he was back on the bench for Saturday's third game of the series.

The Bears took two of the three games in Montreal. Newark continues to charge up the standings, this time at the expense of the Royals, who are now clinging to first place.

No word at press time if Robinson will be back for tonight's doubleheader against Jersey City.

EVERY DAY WHEN MATTHEW left the apartment block, the boys from the street were in one of the alleyways, playing hockey. Most of the time they would be using sticks and a ball, with old boots marking the nets. They never invited Matthew to join them.

"Maybe you have to make the first move," Alain suggested at supper one night, as Matthew poked and prodded at his meatloaf.

"How can I?" Matthew replied. "I don't know a word of French." Which wasn't entirely true. Thanks to all of his time at Delorimier Downs, Matthew now knew quite a bit of French.

"I could help you. I could do the *traduction*—you know, the translation," Alain said kindly, smiling at Grace across the table.

"Yeah, 'cause you sure can't play," Matthew said, then instantly regretted his words.

Alain had lost his foot during the war, and wore a plastic replacement. So he couldn't go out and play hockey with Matthew, even if the boy had wanted him to. Matthew knew this was a horrible thing to say, and he could feel his face getting red as he tried to imagine what Alain must be feeling. The family never mentioned Alain's foot and always tried to pretend that things were normal, even when he took off his replacement or occasionally stumbled.

"I think I'll just wait until school starts next fall," Matthew continued, not lifting his eyes off his plate. He didn't want to see the disappointed look on his mother's face, and he was too ashamed to meet Alain's eyes. Alain shrugged and the hockey players weren't mentioned again.

This was just fine with Matthew. He really didn't want to tell his mother the whole story. Even if he did like playing hockey, he wasn't so sure he'd be welcome. The other boys stopped and stared whenever he went past—and they always seemed to be talking about him. Matthew never got close enough to make out exactly what they were calling him, but he did recognize the word "*anglais*."

It was a sunny day in late June and Matthew was eagerly awaiting the day's game, although he knew Jackie Robinson would be out of the lineup again. The day before, he'd played in a doubleheader against the Newark Bears, but his calf injury seemed to have slowed him down. He hit fifth in the lineup, and went 0–3 in the first game.

And it got worse. He batted only once in the second game.

"Now up for the Royals ... Jackeeeeee Ro-beeeen-son!" Usually Matthew would smile when the stadium announcer made his trademark introduction. Thanks to the man's thick French accent, Jackie Robinson's name took on a few extra vowels. But yesterday, Matthew's forehead had creased with concern as he watched Jackie take his spot at the plate.

"Look at the way he's leaning slightly to one side," Dewey had said. He was walking back to the press box and had stopped to buy some peanuts from Matthew.

Robinson took a big swing and missed. Strike two.

The next pitch was inside. Robinson shifted his stance, trying to get comfortable in his batting position.

Another pitch. Strike three!

Matthew and Dewey had watched as Robinson walked back to the dugout, limping ever so slightly. He frowned as one of the trainers whispered in his ear. They had watched as Jackie got up and followed the trainer into the tunnel.

"He's out of the game again," Dewey had said quietly as they watched the next Royals batter. He told Matthew that some of the newspaper reporters were starting to hint that Robinson couldn't take the pressure of a minor league season, never mind the strain of playing in the major leagues.

Matthew had shaken his head defiantly. Those writers were wrong. Jackie Robinson would make it. Just not today.

He was changing into his uniform when two of the other boys came into the locker room. He was early today, and René hadn't yet arrived.

"Why are you here already, *anglais?*" one of the boys hissed, shoving Matthew up against his locker and holding him there. The other one grabbed Matthew's everyday pants and shook them out.

"No money, there," he snarled. "Maybe in your jacket, then? Hand it over, *p'tit cou!*"

"Get your hands off him." It was Tyrone. The boys dropped Matthew on the bench and scurried out of the locker room.

"Are you okay, son?" Tyrone's voice was a reassuring rumble.

Matthew sighed. "I just don't get it. Why do they pick on me? Just because I'm English!"

Tyrone smiled. "Just ask Jackie Robinson what it's like."

Matthew stared at the old player, waiting for an explanation.

"It's the same thing, isn't it?" Tyrone continued. "Someone doesn't like you because you're different. Different language, different colour skin. Mind you, those boys don't want to kill you. Folks want to kill Jackie Robinson." Tyrone's deep voice was so quiet it was almost a whisper.

"Mr. Rickey wanted to change things." The old man lowered himself onto the bench beside Matthew. "He'd been thinking about this for a long while. Buttering up the Dodgers directors for years to get them to go along with the idea. Jackie was playing in the Negro Leagues back then," Tyrone reminisced. "A Dodger scout named

Clyde Sukeforth showed up to talk to Jackie on Mr. Rickey's behalf. Asked him all the questions he thought Mr. Rickey would want to know. He decided Jackie had the real goods, so he invited him to come with him to Brooklyn to meet Mr. Rickey."

Tyrone paused, with a smile. "Mr. Rickey, he tested Jackie pretty good," he chuckled. "Asked him first of all if he had a girl. Guess he wanted a solid fellow, not someone out chasing skirts."

Matthew tried not to giggle as Tyrone continued. "Then he asked Jackie what he'd do in all kinds of situations. If a hotel clerk tried to insult him. Or if a player badmouths him during a game. Or even takes a swing at him."

Tyrone put his hands on his hips and pretended he was puffing on a cigar, doing his own imitation of Branch Rickey. "'Jackie,' Mr. Rickey said, 'suppose I'm a player in the heat of an important game. And I collide with you at second base and then I call you a dirty black son of a.... What do you do?'"

The old man chuckled. "He did that to Jackie over and over again. He even tried to land a punch on him. And Jackie didn't flinch, and didn't budge an inch. I guess Mr. Rickey had found his man. Jackie had all the right answers, I suppose," continued Tyrone. "He asked Mr. Rickey, 'Are you looking for someone who would not have the courage to fight back?'"

"And Mr. Rickey, sure as I'm standing right here, do you know what he said? He told Jackie, 'I am looking for someone with the courage *not* to fight back.'"

Tyrone paused for a moment to let his words sink in. Matthew looked at the old black ballplayer with amazement. How could Tyrone know all of this?

"But Tyrone, how do you—"

He waved his hand at Matthew. "I've told you too much already, boy. René knows this story, but don't you go tellin' anybody else. Y'hear? You'll find out all you need to know in good time, boy." And quickly, for an old man, he slid out of the locker room.

With Robinson out of the lineup, the Royals had lost to Newark 9–7. Still, it had been a good game, and Matthew was feeling happy as he made his way home. As he walked, he noticed the streets of Montreal were alive with the sights and sounds of summer. There were colourful strings of laundry hanging across many of the balconies and boxes of fresh produce outside all the local *épiceries*, or grocery stores. As he walked by open windows, he caught bits and pieces of the favourite *téléroman*, the French soap operas that were all the rage on the radio. And at the *dépanneur*, the sports pages of the Montreal newspapers were filled with stories of Jackie Robinson and speculation as to when he would rejoin his team.

As always, Matthew was carrying his baseball glove and a ball. He tossed the ball in the air and caught it in his glove as he walked along the street.

"You like baseball?"

Matthew paused on the steps of his building. He turned to see a boy standing in the alleyway, holding a hockey stick and ball. Although Matthew had seen him many times before, playing hockey with the others, he was not one of the ones who had been laughing or calling him "*anglais.*" In fact, Matthew had always thought the boy looked a little sad.

"Yeah, I used to play a lot back home," Matthew replied. He was surprised at how well the boy spoke English. He had always assumed that the hockey boys knew only French.

"Where are you from?" the boy continued, putting down his ball and stick and settling onto the concrete railing that led to the building.

"We used to live in Pembroke. It's in Ontario," said Matthew, sitting down on one of the steps, across from the boy.

"Oh. Me? We come from a farm in the Eastern Townships. *Tu le connais?* There are lots of English people around there," the boy answered, as if explaining to Matthew why he spoke so well.

"*Je m'appelle Guy,*" the boy added, flashing a toothy grin. He was a bit taller than Matthew and had jet black hair and brown eyes. Matthew noticed that Guy's jeans had been patched many times and his T-shirt was wearing thin.

"I'm Matthew."

"So why didn't you come to our school?" Guy asked. As he spoke, Guy kept one eye on a window above.

Matthew shrugged. "I don't know much French, and I'd already finished most of the year in Ontario. So my mom and Alain—that's my stepfather—they said I could wait until September."

"*Mais tu parles bien maintenant*," Guy said. "I've heard you speaking French with your *père*. You'll be fine."

Matthew gave the boy a grateful look. He was having some doubts about what it would be like to go to school. He spoke plenty of French now, especially at the ballpark. But he still wasn't sure he would fit in.

"My father, he was killed in the war," Guy continued. "It's just me and Maman now."

Matthew didn't know what to say. He thought about the people back in Pembroke who had also lost a father or brother during the war. One of his teachers at elementary school had enlisted when the war began. He had been killed at the big battle at Normandy two years ago. Several of the young clerks at the grocery store had been killed there, too. Many others had come back to town bearing the scars of war. Matthew would see them around Pembroke, legs and arms missing—so different from how they had looked like before they left.

Guy took another anxious look up at the window. "I have to go soon. Maman takes me to work with her and sometimes I help out at the factory. It gives us a few more dollars. One more year of school and I'll be able to get a job for good."

Matthew was surprised. Guy couldn't be more than one or two years older than he was. How could he be talking about dropping out of school?

A woman stuck her head out the window. "*Cinq minutes, Guy! Viens vite!*"

"I've got to go," Guy said, getting up and picking up his stick and ball.

"Can you teach me and my friends how to play ball someday? All we ever play is hockey."

"Sure," Matthew replied. Guy gave Matthew a small wave as he sprinted for the back stairs and disappeared from sight.

Matthew told his mother and Alain about his new friend at supper. His mom was also surprised when he told them that Guy was thinking of leaving school.

Alain shrugged. "That's the reality, I suppose. If his mother can't afford for him to go to college, there's no use for him to stay in school. He's better off going out and getting a trade, something to make a living."

"And speaking of college ...." His mother smiled. "Alain has some news."

SO LONG, JACKIE ROBINSON    91

Matthew was surprised to see his stepfather blush.

"Yes, it's true. I am going back to school. Can you believe it? At my age?"

"It's wonderful news." His wife smiled. "Alain is going to finish his high school and then he's been accepted into teacher's college."

"I guess I'm a bit like Guy," Alain explained. "I left school to go work in a factory with my uncle and my cousins. I always said I'd go back to the classroom some day, but never got the chance. Then came the war."

"Now the government is helping veterans to get their education," Grace said proudly.

"It's going to be a big adjustment. You know, back to the books after so many years. I hope you'll help me out, Matthieu." Alain gave his stepson a shy look.

"Uh, I don't know. I'll be kind of busy," Matthew stuttered. He could feel his mother's eyes on him, willing him to be nice to his stepfather.

"Ah, *oui*," said Alain, obviously disappointed. He picked up his plate and left the room. Grace didn't say a word but Matthew could tell by her expression that she wasn't happy with him.


The next day at the ballpark, Matthew had his eyes peeled for any sign of Jackie Robinson.

"I hear he's going to be back in the lineup this afternoon," René told him as the boys quickly loaded up their baskets before the game.

"What about his pulled muscle?" Matthew asked.

René shrugged. "That's the word. He's going to try to play. He's probably tired of reading all that stuff about himself in the papers."

"You mean, him being a quitter?"

"*Oui*. How he's not such a great ballplayer after all. He's got bad ankles. Bad knees. Everything. Even Monsieur Hopper said Jackie's legs are not holding up," whispered René, looking around to make sure no one was listening. "He said Jackie had missed so many games because of his legs."

"But I read in the paper that his leg was black and blue," Matthew jumped to Jackie's defence. "And all the players have been asking him how he's doing every day. I've seen them. They don't seem to think he's faking it."

René shrugged his shoulders. "I heard Tyrone talking about it with one of the bosses. They were telling him to have a talk with Jackie. I guess they're not convinced he's really hurt. Or if he is hurt, they want him to get better fast."

"Why Tyrone?"

But René didn't get a chance to answer. All at once, he grabbed Matthew's arm and pulled him down behind the counter. Wrestling his arm free, Matthew peeked over the edge. Tyrone was making his way down the corridor, and with him was none other than Jackie

Robinson—in full uniform.

The two boys strained to hear what the old ballplayer was saying to the famous rookie.

"You don't have to do it, son." They heard Tyrone's unmistakable rumble.

The boys exchanged looks of surprise and René put his finger over lips. Matthew nodded. He was barely breathing.

"I know what I should do, Ty, but it just gets to be too much sometimes. For Rachel, I mean."

"Well, if you think it's too much for Rachel, you just say so. But I ain't never heard her say that. You know what I'm sayin'? So it all comes down to you," the old man concluded.

In the distance, the boys could hear the murmur of the first spectators making their way to their seats. Whatever Tyrone and Jackie Robinson were talking about, they were going to have to finish up soon.

"You're right, Ty. I'll do it. For Rachel. And for you."

Matthew looked at his friend and raised his eyebrow. What was Jackie Robinson talking about?

Tyrone laughed and Matthew heard the sound of his hand slapping the young ballplayer on the back. "You're doin' it for all of us and for yourself. But whenever it gets to be too much, you come talk to me and I'll remind you how it used to be. Now you get out there and show them how the game is played."

When the coast was clear, the two friends slid out from their hiding spots and finished loading peanuts and popcorn.

"It's going to be some game, eh!" René said with a grin.

"You betcha!" Matthew replied.

And it was. With Robinson back in the lineup, after missing all but two games since the end of May, the Royals split a doubleheader with Jersey City. But that was just the beginning. All in all, the team took four out of five games against the Giants, outscoring their opponents 49–14.

The next day, the boys were back at the ballpark again. Now the Royals were taking on their rivals from Baltimore, and there always seemed to be trouble when the two teams met.

"At least here Jackie doesn't have to worry about the crowd trying to attack him," Matthew whispered to René as they stood waiting for the national anthems to end.

"But what about the players? They've got a bad reputation for making it rough on Jackie," René replied.

"He's tough. That much we know!" Matthew responded. The two boys headed out as the umpire yelled, "Play ball!"

Jackie Robinson got a big cheer from the crowd when his name was announced in the starting lineup.

"On second base, Jack-eeeeeee Ro-beeeen-son!"

There was an even bigger response when Jackie came up to bat. He was back in his familiar spot, batting second. And he didn't disappoint the crowd, getting a hit in his first at-bat.

A large man with a head of thick white hair slicked back with Brylcreem bellowed out, "Jackie, 'e's my boy!" in a thick French accent. The fan, with a big beer belly and a Royals flag in one hand, always yelled the same thing. But this time, Matthew could almost swear he saw a smile dance across Jackie Robinson's face when the old man yelled.

Mid-way through the game, Matthew and René went to restock their trays with peanuts and popcorn. Jackie now had several hits. And he'd proven that his leg was in good shape with a clever steal in the fourth.

Then, in the fifth, Robinson was on third when Spider Jorgensen came up to bat. Jackie took a big lead and started his trademark dance up and down the baseline. Jersey City pitcher Phil Oates threw to third, but Jackie got back safely. Then, on the first pitch, Jackie broke for home. He stopped halfway and scrambled back to base. It was a move that he'd used in the opening game of the season against Jersey City and the Montreal crowd roared with approval. Jackie repeated the dance along the base path on every pitch. Finally, Oates was so thrown off that he balked and Robinson was awarded home plate! The Royals now had a five-run lead.

"I guess his leg is really better," Matthew said to his friend with a smile.

"Let's hope it stays that way," René replied. "I'm going over to see Tyrone." He pointed to the next section where the old ballplayer was standing with a big grin on his face.

A few minutes later, Matthew was passing a bag of popcorn to one of the Royals' fans when the man gasped and started waving at the field.

"*C'est pas correct, là!*"

"What happened?" Matthew asked in French. "*Qu'est-ce qui est arrivé?*"

"*Il a frappé Jackie Robinson quand il est arrivé au deuxième but,*" the man replied.

Matthew was astonished. The Baltimore player had hit Jackie Robinson in the middle of the game, in front of sixteen thousand fans? He gave the man his change and raced over to where René was standing with Tyrone.

"Did you see it?" Matthew gasped.

"The nerve of that fella," Tyrone fumed. "He ran right into Jackie and gave him a kick in the back. Plain as plain could be."

The Royals' fans were on their feet yelling at the umpire. It had been a forced out, so the Baltimore player was out before he even got to second base.

The crowd showed no sign of letting up. The umpire

walked over to first base to confer with the other officials. Robinson was brushing himself off, while the
Baltimore player was already back in the Orioles'
dugout, joking with some of his teammates. Finally, the
umpire went back to home base and started putting his
equipment back on.

"Play ball!" he barked.

The fans kept on shouting. Suddenly, Robinson
headed across the diamond, jogging his way to home
base. The umpire seemed caught off guard and froze, his
mask halfway up to his face.

No one in the ballpark could hear what the two were
saying, but Robinson was waving his hands around, as if
trying to describing what happened. The umpire listened carefully and sent him back to second base. Then,
he went down to the dugout and had a brief conversation with the Baltimore manager. The player who had
run into Jackie Robinson was now sitting at the end of
the Orioles' bench, away from the rest of the team. The
other players obviously didn't approve of what their
teammate had done.

"That's the spirit, boy," Tyrone said with a pleased
look on his face. "He doesn't have to just take that. He
stood up for himself. That's the way to do it."

"But what can the umpire do?" Matthew asked.

"Not much, boy, not much," the old ballplayer replied.
"The fact that Jackie made his case and the umpire

listened was good. But for the ump to go and say something to the manager, that was even better. That's telling all the players to keep their hands off Jackie Robinson."

"Will it work?" René wondered.

"No, it won't make much difference next time they go to Baltimore or another city like it. But for today, sure, it might help. Sure."

Matthew wished he had time to continue his talk with Tyrone. He wanted to ask the man about his earlier conversation with Jackie. But they had to get back to work. And besides, Matthew didn't really want the old ballplayer to know he'd been spying on him.

After the game, as they changed out of their uniforms, Matthew and René talked more about what they had seen.

"Tyrone said he knew one of the Royals players in the Negro Leagues," Matthew suggested.

"It's Jackie, for sure," René agreed. "But why is Jackie Robinson doing this for him? For Tyrone?"

Matthew shook his head. "Could they have played together? Was Tyrone his coach?"

"Tyrone seems pretty important to Jackie," René nodded. "But more important than a coach or teammate, don't you think?"

Matthew nodded, but before they could say any more, they heard the voices of the other vendors headed for the locker room. The boys quickly ducked out of the second door and back into the summer sunshine. The mystery of Tyrone and Jackie Robinson would have to wait.

# Chapter Eight

# Mr. Rickey Comes to Town

## Robinson Impressive in Royals' Road Trip

by Dewey Barton

*July 7, 1946*

After four doubleheaders in seven days, the Montreal Royals can be forgiven for wondering where they are and who they're playing.

The Royals took game one of their latest doubleheader against the Toronto Maple Leafs, 8–5.

Game two was tied, 2–2, when it was called to allow the teams to catch trains.

Toronto and Montreal will play yet another doubleheader today at Delorimier Downs.

Robinson now has nineteen runs in sixteen games since returning from his leg injury.

Rumours abound that Brooklyn Dodgers head honcho Branch Rickey will be in town for today's doubleheader.

JUNE MELTED INTO JULY. The streets of Montreal were sweltering and the local YMCA was the most popular place in Matthew's neighbourhood. Many of the kids spent entire days there, dipping in and out of the pool. Matthew was too shy to go by himself and it was too far for René to come and join him. Meanwhile, Guy was working long hours at the factory with his mother and had no time for summer fun.

Matthew was now living in the heart of a big city, and gone were the days when he and A.J. could run off to the fishing hole for a cool swim. Actually, Matthew rarely thought about his home back in Pembroke anymore. He had written a few letters to A.J. and his friend had written back. But it wasn't the same. He didn't even know how the Beavers were doing this season! School was over now and the boys would be spending all their time at the ball diamond. He felt a pang of guilt as he remembered how disappointed A.J. had been that the best pitching duo in the Pembroke ball league was breaking up. It all seemed far away now.

These days, Matthew's whole world consisted of his apartment, and the Royals ballpark, and the walk in between. While his mother and Alain had initially been enthusiastic about Matthew's job, he got the sense they were starting to change their minds.

"Why don't you spend more time with the kids your age, here in the neighbourhood?" his mother urged. "We don't need the money, you know. We can even pay you an allowance, if that would help."

"You're just twelve," Alain added. "You should be enjoying your summer. Goodness knows, there is enough hard work ahead of you. Be a kid."

"I am being a kid—I'm a kid who loves baseball," Matthew replied coolly. "I love it there. And besides, I'm learning lots of French. Wasn't that the idea?"

"Yes, I'm sure you are. I'm just not sure what kind of French you're learning," his stepfather said grimly.

"And this whole Jackie Robinson thing," his mother added. "Alain, is Matt even safe there? I keep hearing about all the controversy and all the threats."

"That's not here, Mom," Matthew answered angrily. He'd explained this to her before. Why couldn't she get it? "The Montreal fans love Jackie Robinson. They're always chanting '*Allez, allez, allez!*' whenever he's on base because they want him to steal another. And lots of times he does. Some people say Jackie's as popular as Rocket Richard."

Despite his earlier anger, Alain burst out laughing. "Oh, I'd believe it, too. Montreal fans love a winner and there's no doubt Jackie Robinson is going to be a winner. Maybe even lead the Royals to the pennant."

Before Matthew could say anything more, his mother interrupted.

"Alain, before Matt heads to the ballpark, we should

tell him the good news."

Matthew looked from his mother to his stepfather. What good news?

"You and I are heading to Pembroke for a visit!" his mother exclaimed. "Grandma and Grandpa miss you so much. They've sent us money for our bus tickets."

"Ummm, when?" Matthew asked. He noticed that his mother looked disappointed that he wasn't more excited. "I mean, I can't wait! When do we go?"

"Tomorrow," his mother replied. "So you'd better get your things packed up tonight after the game."

"We wanted it to be a surprise," Alain explained.

"Great," Matthew said quietly. "May I be excused? I, uh, need to pack."

Matthew could feel his mother's eyes watching him as he left the room. He quietly closed the door to his bedroom and sank onto the bed.

He tried to understand what he was feeling. His stomach was churning, as if he was going to throw up.

"I'm going home," he whispered, trying out the words to see how they felt.

He looked around his room. His baseball glove had a place of honour on a shelf, surrounded by the trophies he had won with A.J. There was a picture, too, from last summer. Matthew walked over, picked it up and looked closely at his best friend. What would it be like to see A.J. again? Would A.J. even care that he was back?

Then he thought about what he was going to be missing. He picked up the Royals schedule for July from its spot on his desk. "Phew!" he said, "They're on the road for the two whole weeks." He didn't want to miss too many games, though it seemed inevitable that he would miss some. And what would Tyrone think? The old ballplayer had gone out of his way to help Matthew fit in at Delorimier Downs. And what about René? How were they ever going to solve the mystery of the relationship between Tyrone and Jackie?

Matthew felt a surge of frustration. Why couldn't his parents leave things alone? Why did they have to keep changing his life? He glanced at the clock. No time to start packing. He had to get to the ballpark.

When he arrived at Delorimier Downs, the crew was already hard at work. There had been rain that morning and everyone was scrambling to get the field ready for the game. Matthew looked around the ballpark, hoping to spot Tyrone. No luck. He had to settle for heading down to the lockers, where René was already getting changed.

"Is something wrong, *ami?*" he asked as Matthew rummaged around in his locker. "You haven't said a word since you arrived."

When Matthew didn't answer, René kept on talking. "We need to keep an eye out for Monsieur Rickey," he continued, his eyes sparkling with excitement. "Maybe the rumours are true and he will be bringing Jackie to the big leagues very soon."

There had been talk that the Dodgers were thinking of calling Robinson up. He now seemed to be fully recovered from his leg injury and was burning up the International League with hits and stolen bases.

Matthew didn't know what to say. Not only was he was going to miss the weekend series, he didn't even know how long he would be away!

"Oh great," he moaned, sinking onto the bench and putting his head in his hands.

"Matthieu, what's wrong?" René's voice was full of concern. *"Qu'est-ce qu'arrive?"*

"It's such a mess," Matthew began. "My mom is taking me home to Pembroke and I don't want to go. But I can't tell her. And just a few weeks ago, before I started working here, all I wanted was to go home! I don't know when I'll be back. And what about Jackie Robinson? If he gets called up, I'll never see him again!"

"Whoa, boy," a voice boomed into the locker room. Matthew and René turned to see Tyrone's head poking through the door. "Did I hear you say Jackie Robinson's heading to the big leagues? And he didn't tell me? The sass of that boy!"

The big man walked into the room, slapping his thigh in pretend exasperation and making both boys laugh.

"No, Tyrone." Matthew smiled, in spite of himself. "It's just me. I have to go home—I mean, to Pembroke—for a while. And I'm afraid of what I'm going to miss here."

"Well, boy, we'll miss you, too," said Tyrone. "But Jackie's still going to be here when you get back. Don't you worry none. Maybe next season he'll head to Brooklyn. But he's staying right here for now.

"And you know, things are going better here for Jackie," Tyrone continued. The old ballplayer pulled off his cap and wiped the sweat from his forehead.

"What do you mean?" asked René.

"Well, when the season started, Jackie, he'd be by himself all the time on the road," explained Tyrone. "Except if Miss Rachel was there. But he didn't have nothin' to do with the rest of the boys."

Tyrone smiled. "But then, one day, Al, he up and asked Jackie to sit at his table at lunch."

Matthew and René exchanged glances. Tyrone meant Al Campanis, the shortstop. The ballplayer had always seemed the friendliest with Jackie on the field as well—which made sense because they played in such close proximity to each other.

"Now, Jackie's even started playing cards with the rest of the boys," Tyrone said, shaking his head. "Never thought I'd see the day."

Tyrone's news was wonderful, but it made Matthew wonder what else he was going to miss while he was away.

"What about my job?" Matthew asked anxiously. "Cecile is going to fire me."

"Now, you just let me deal with Cecile," Tyrone grinned. "That girl, she does like me a lot. So I'll just sweeten her up. And she'll be all set to welcome you back. Don't you worry none about that. You worry about spending time with your mama and doing the right thing by her."

Outside the locker room door, the first announcements boomed over the loudspeaker, and then voices of Royals fans could be heard in the corridor.

"You boys get goin'," Tyrone urged. "I've got to go check on Jackie."

The boys finished dressing in silence. As they left the locker room, Matthew realized that René hadn't said a word about his trip to Pembroke.

The boys ducked and weaved through the corridors under the stadium—corridors that they now knew like the back of their hands. Only the staff could use the narrow tunnels that snaked around the big ballpark and Matthew always felt a surge of excitement when he was using the secret passageways, like he was one of the insiders.

"Are you mad at me, René?" Matthew asked as they headed down the hallway to pick up their supplies.

René paused to think. "Not mad. Just surprised."

"Surprised?" Matthew replied. "At what?"

"That you were so unhappy here."

"No, you don't get it." Matthew stopped his friend. "Not now. Not since I came here. Not since I met you. But before, I was lonely. I didn't know anyone. I didn't speak French. All the kids in the neighbourhood called me '*anglais.*' I missed my grandparents. And my friends. And baseball."

The boys turned as they heard the crack of a bat against a ball. Batting practice had started.

"Now I have it all. Baseball and friends." Matthew smiled at René.

"And you're not bad for an *anglais.*" René gave his friend a nudge.

Matthew was serious for a minute. "Why did you become friends with me? I mean all the other kids, they didn't want anything to do with me because I'm English. Why didn't it bother you?"

René shrugged. "I guess I know what it's like to be different."

Suddenly, the boys heard their names called. "*Vite. Vite. Le jeu commence!*"

Only later did Matthew have time to stop and think about what his friend had said. What made René different? Matthew thought back to the first time he had met his friend. The boy had been quietly changing, away from the louder group of teenagers. It was as if he somehow didn't fit in. But René was French, Matthew thought.

He wasn't different at all. He wished he'd had a chance to ask René about it. Now he'd have to wait until he returned from Pembroke. Whenever that would be.

The crowd was abuzz this afternoon. The rumours were flying that Jackie Robinson was heading up to play for the Dodgers. Matthew saw the reporters, including Dewey Barton and Sam Hill, swarming around a man in a suit and a fedora: Branch Rickey.

Throughout the game, Matthew tried to keep an eye on Rickey, almost tripping several times as he walked past the manager's box. Rachel Robinson was also in the box, fanning herself with a program. She was now noticeably pregnant, making her even more conspicuous in the primarily all-white stands. Matthew noticed that Mrs. Robinson wore a worried look on her face for most of the game. He wondered if she felt the same pressure as her husband.

On the field, there was plenty of excitement. The big crowd was clearly behind their Royals, especially as they faced off against their Canadian rivals from Toronto. Branch Rickey had arrived just as the second game of the doubleheader was about to begin. Matthew wished that the Dodgers' head honcho had been in the stands for the first game. It had been a good one for Jackie. He went 2 for 4 at the plate, and had finally managed to steal another base—his first in more than a dozen games. Now, though, the pressure was on. Matthew could only imagine how much Jackie wanted to impress the man who had staked his career on Robinson's performance.

In the third inning, Jackie was up, with a chance to give the Royals the lead. The big ballplayer seemed nervous. He swung awkwardly at the first two pitches, and then popped up on the third. Robinson was done, without even making it on base to show off his trademark running style for Mr. Rickey.

The Maple Leafs started hitting in the middle innings and the game was quickly tied 2–2.

"This is your chance, Jackie," Matthew whispered as the rookie took his place at the plate. The Royals had a runner on base. Robinson could tie the game or, better yet, give his team the lead.

"Take it easy, now," said René quietly. He had snuck over from section D where he had been assigned for the afternoon. Matthew had drawn the coveted centre rows right behind home plate. Both boys were quiet, as was the rest of the crowd, sensing this was the moment the Royals' star had been waiting for.

Robinson seemed more patient this at-bat.

He let one ball go by. And another. Ball two. Every time, Robinson carefully set up at the plate, his powerful legs bent at the knees, his strong arms and wrists lightly wielding the bat. The Maple Leafs pitcher seemed to be tiring. It was the perfect scenario for a home run.

Jackie took a big swing at the next pitch and just missed.

"Oh, that would have been a home run!" René exclaimed. "Encore!"

"I think he's trying too hard," said Matthew. He recalled how he felt when he was up at bat back in Pembroke and wanted desperately to hit a home run. It never seemed to work the way he wanted it to. Then, he shook away the thought. After all, this was Jackie Robinson.

The count was two balls, one strike now as Jackie got set. The pitcher shook off a couple of signals from his catcher and then got ready to throw.

Jackie made good contact with the ball. But it went foul—way off into the right-field stands.

The next pitch was a ball. The count was full. Matthew looked around at the fans who were hanging on every pitch, every swing. They were all hoping for an exciting finish for their team.

The pitcher wound up, and let go. Jackie swung and popped the ball high into the air. The pitcher waved off his catcher as he set up under the ball. It plopped into his glove. He waved it triumphantly at the fans as Robinson, his body stiff as a board, returned to the Royals' dugout.

"Well, at least he got an RBI," Matthew whispered to

René. But they both knew it wasn't the kind of performance Robinson would have wanted in front of Branch Rickey. The rest of the game went the same way. Jackie had one or two good fielding plays, but was hitless, with just the one run batted in. No stolen bases.

Thankfully, the rest of the team fared better. The game ended in a 5–2 victory and the fans cheered loudly as the two teams jogged off the field, as if trying to impress the Dodgers' boss with their support. Matthew and René watched as Jackie left the field with his teammates. His head was bowed slightly, and he was moving slower than usual.

The stands were empty now. The wind gently blew the peanut shells and empty popcorn wrappers that Matthew and the others were now picking up all around the giant stadium.

"Some game, eh kid?"

Dewey Barton walked by, carrying his big camera.

"I don't think Jackie Robinson would say that," Matthew replied.

The reporter laughed. "Oh, sure, everyone was hoping he'd go 3-for-3 at the plate, make clutch plays every inning and hit a couple of home runs to boot."

"Sir?"

Dewey sat down on a bench for a second, lifted his hat, and wiped his brow.

"Even Branch Rickey said it after the game. He said,

sure, it wasn't Jackie's best game ever, but there's still plenty of season left. And one game is just that—one game."

"Do you believe that?" Matthew asked timidly.

The young reporter shrugged. "I guess if you're Jackie Robinson there is nothing but pressure. So he messes up a few at-bats. He can't let that get him down. And he hasn't let anything stop him so far this season."

Matthew thought about the rumours surrounding Robinson's leg injury and wondered if the reporter wasn't trying to paint a positive picture of what had been a very disappointing performance by the man that they both admired.

Matthew remembered what Tyrone had said. "Does this mean Jackie's not going up to play for the Dodgers?"

Dewey shook his head. "I don't think this game will make a difference one way or another. Branch Rickey has a plan. This is the first part of it. Only he knows when the second step will be.

"But I think it's better for Jackie to stay here for the season," the reporter continued.

"Better than playing in the big leagues?" Matthew was surprised.

"Look at the way he's treated now," Dewey explained. "It's enough pressure playing for the little ol' Montreal Royals. Imagine playing for the Dodgers! That's pressure for any player, never mind the first-ever Negro player.

"How much can one man take?" Dewey asked. "Mr.

Rickey wants to make sure Jackie's good and ready, because they're only going to get one chance at this."

"Why just one chance?" Matthew persisted.

Dewey shrugged. "Because if things go wrong for Jackie or the Dodgers, the ones who hate Negroes will say, 'We told you so. They're not fit for the major leagues.' And that will ruin it for all the black fellas who want to follow."

Dewey smiled. "It's complicated stuff, Matt. I'm not sure I get it some days."

The reporter got back to his feet. "Well, I better get going. See you tomorrow."

"Umm, you won't," Matthew said quietly. "I'm heading ho ... to Pembroke for a couple of weeks."

Dewey looked surprised. "I thought your folks were settled here?"

"Oh, sure," said Matthew. "It's just a little holiday. To see my grandparents. I'll be back."

"Well, see ya when I see ya, kid." Dewey tipped his hat at Matthew. "Keep practising that fastball."

As he packed that night, Matthew carefully laid his baseball glove on top of his suitcase. He wore the glove all the time, on his way to and from the stadium, but he couldn't remember the last time he'd used it to practise, or to play with another kid. He suddenly felt a surge of anger. He had been spending all his time watching other people play ball. Now he was going to face his friends, who had been spending their whole summer on the diamond.

Matthew tossed and turned all night, worrying about the trip ahead. When he did finally fall into a troubled sleep, he dreamed that he was at the plate, facing a mean-looking Orioles pitcher, with a hissing black cat up on the mound next to him. And like Jackie Robinson today, Matthew kept striking out.

# Chapter Nine

## *Where is Home?*

**Robinson Boosts Batting Average**
by Dewey Barton
*July 22, 1946*
Jackie Robinson had a pair of hits in a doubleheader sweep in Syracuse yesterday.

Robinson boosted his average from .344 to .349, thanks in part to a solo homer in the nightcap.

Meanwhile, the Royals extended their lead to 15 games.

MATTHEW COULD FEEL HIS HEART pounding as the bus rolled across the familiar countryside just outside of Pembroke. His mother sat across the aisle from him, dropping in and out of sleep.

He wondered what was going on with his mother these days. She seemed to be sleeping a lot—and Alain had insisted that she take a bagful of snacks, even though she said she was feeling a little queasy about being on a bus for six hours.

Matthew had brought along the three letters that A.J. had written to him since he left Pembroke. He smiled as he looked at his friend's messy handwriting. He could picture A.J. hunched over the paper, trying to be neat but never quite succeeding.

Matthew frowned as he read one of the last paragraphs—about the Beavers and their new coach. Matthew knew Timmy Riley but couldn't really remember his father. Bud Riley had been overseas since the war began and this was his first season coaching.

"Coach Riley is really strict," A.J. had written. "It's not as much fun as when you were here."

He looked out the window as the bus rolled through the lush green fields of the Ottawa Valley, trying to imagine what the team must be like this year. Well, he'd be able to ask A.J. soon enough.

Now his mother stirred and gave Matthew a smile. "We're almost here, Mattie," she said softly. She hardly ever used his old nickname anymore and hearing it made Matthew perk up, despite his nerves.

The bus turned off the highway and headed towards the downtown section of the city. Matthew could see the red bricks of City Hall up ahead and all the familiar shops along Main Street.

"There's Grandma and Grandpa," cried his mother,

waving as the bus pulled into the station.

"You go first," she urged her son.

But Matthew stood back shyly and mumbled, "No, you."

He followed his mother off the bus. Grace threw herself into her mother's arms, tears rolling down her face.

"I'm so happy for you," Matthew heard his grandmother say, gently stroking her daughter's hair. "How was the trip? We should get you home. You'll need to rest."

"And who is this fine looking gentleman?" said a booming voice from behind Matthew. He turned to see his grandfather holding their bags.

"I'd shake hands, fine sir, but my hands are full," his grandpa grinned. Then he put down the bags and reached out his arms. Matthew was instantly caught up in a huge bear hug.

"Let me see him, John," Annabel Parker said, nudging her husband aside. "Oh, you've grown so! And you are truly the picture of your father."

Annabel looked up at her daughter. "I'm sorry, Gracie. Was that the wrong thing to say?"

"No, Mama, no," Matthew's mom answered, wiping the tears from her eyes. "He is. I can see it so much more here. We'll have to get out some old pictures, eh?"

The rest of the afternoon was a blur of emotions for Matthew. His old room was exactly as he had left it. It felt so familiar, but so strange at the same time. He looked around at the empty shelves where his books and trophies had been. He unpacked his suitcase, and put his glove on the bedside table, where he'd always kept it.

When he came downstairs, his mother was curled up on the living room couch under a blanket.

"There's nothing like a nap on my favourite couch in the world to make me feel better," she whispered to Matthew, who settled into a chair and started flipping through a magazine.

"And so, what do you think of the news?" Matthew's grandmother asked as she swished in with a tray of tea and cookies. Matthew smiled as he saw his favourite mug brimming with hot chocolate. Who cared if it was the middle of summer?

"Mother!" Grace said quickly.

Matthew turned and gave his grandmother a puzzled look.

"Oh," Grandma said, putting her hand over her mouth. "I've let the cat out of the bag."

Matthew's mother sat up and patted the seat next to her on the couch. She waited for Matthew to join her before she continued.

"I was waiting until we got here to tell you, Mattie," she said softly. Matthew felt his stomach lurch. What was wrong?

"Oh, don't look so worried," she smiled. "It's good news. You're going to have a brother or sister."

She put her hand on her belly. "That's why I've been

so tired lately. The baby is due around Christmas."

Matthew stared blankly at his mother, not sure what to say or do.

"Give me a hug, you big boy of mine," his grandmother said, taking his hand and pulling him up from the couch. "I want you to tell me all about your adventures in Montreal. And this ball team I've been hearing so much about."

Matthew turned back to his mother. He could feel her watching him, waiting for him to say something.

"That's great news, Mom," he said quietly. "I'm really happy for you and Alain."

He knew it wasn't exactly what she wanted to hear, but it was all he could muster. As he left the room with his grandmother, his mother lay back down, her hands resting gently on her belly, a smile on her face.


"A.J. Kirkpatrick has been asking about you," his grandfather said later. He and Matthew were out in the yard, trimming back the hedges. "I think he's going to stop by after the ball game. Unless you'd like to go to the game?" Pop stopped clipping. Matthew paused too.

"I don't know, Pop," Matthew replied. "It feels kind of weird. Like I belong here, but I don't. And to see my team ..." His voice trailed off.

"But you do like Montreal, don't you?" Pop said in a casual voice, as he got back to his clipping.

"Yeah, it's okay," Matthew sighed. "I mean, I love the Royals and my friends at the ballpark. And Jackie Robinson is so amazing! All the stuff he's been through. And I have this friend, Tyrone, and he's friends with Jackie Robinson. And my friend René taught me the ropes at the ball field. And there's this boy named Guy and he lives at our apartment block and he has to go to work next year even though he's just a year older than me."

Pop burst into laughter. "Well, for a place that's just 'okay,' you sure seem to be fitting in just fine."

Matthew smiled and looked at his feet. "It's not that. It's just scary sometimes because everyone speaks French and I'm still learning. And some of the kids in the neighbourhood, they don't like anybody who's *anglais*." Matthew paused. "And then, you know, there's Mom and Alain. And now a baby. I just feel sometimes like I'm in the way."

Pop wiped his brow and motioned for Matthew to sit down with him on the back step.

"It's always difficult when things change," Pop said in a serious voice. "And your mom, she's been through a lot of changes. A lot of them really tough ones. When your father was killed, she used to say that she would never be happy again. But then, you came along. And how could she not be happy once she saw you? And she was happy. But we always knew that there was something missing. Someone to share all those special moments with."

"But what about you and Grandma? We shared them with you!" Matthew argued.

"And I wouldn't trade those moments for the world," Pop said, his eyes glistening. "I was so busy when your mother and Aunt Judy were growing up that I missed a lot of those special times. But I got to share them with you. You were my second chance."

Matthew nodded. "So Alain is Mom's second chance? And the baby?"

Pop gave him a gentle smile. "And you. You're going to be a family now. If that's what you want."

"What do you mean, if that's what I want?"

"Well, your mother thinks you're unhappy in Montreal. And so we've offered to have you stay here with us," he paused. "If that's what you want."

Matthew's mind was racing. It was a lot to take in. What did he really want to do?

"So what about that ball game?" Pop said, changing the subject.

"Sure!" Matthew said jumping up from the porch. "I'm going to bring my glove. Just in case."

Matthew squirmed on the hard wooden benches at the Riverside Ballpark. He was having a hard time concentrating on the game.

When he and Pop arrived, his friends were out on the diamond warming up. Matthew gave them a wave, and a few of the boys waved back. A.J. Kirkpatrick started running toward his friend, but was waved back by Coach Riley.

"Keep yer mind on the game," the coach yelled at the boys. "This is for first place—where we should have been all season long. Now get back to work."

Matthew and his grandfather found two seats behind the backstop. He was glad that they weren't within eye range of the Beavers dugout. He got the feeling the coach wasn't too happy to see him at the game. But why?

The Beavers got off to a bad start. The Renfrew team scored three runs in the first inning and Matthew and his grandfather could hear Coach Riley roaring from the dugout.

"Do you need glasses, son? How could you have missed that ball?"

"And you, Kirkpatrick, quit the lollygagging. You could have got that little runt out. Move next time!"

By the fourth inning, Renfrew was ahead 8–2. No matter who pitched for the Beavers, the Renfrew players just kept hitting.

"Do you wish you were out there?" Pop said softly to Matthew.

Matthew shook his head, no. He noticed some of the parents looking over at him and whispering to each other.

The game ended with Renfrew winning 8–3. The dejected Beavers gave a weak cheer and then returned to the dugout, where Coach Riley continued to spew criticism at his players. Everyone in the stands could hear.

Donny Kirkpatrick, A.J.'s father, came over and shook hands with Pop.

"Welcome back, Matthew. They sure could use you this year."

"What's going on with Bud Riley?" Pop asked, lowering his voice. "I'm not sure he needs to be yelling at the boys like that. This is not the major leagues."

Donny shrugged. "He's been like that all season long. The team hasn't been winning the way it used to. His son took over as pitcher, and it just hasn't worked out. Someone told me that Bud used to dream of a spot in the major leagues. He didn't make it. Maybe he hopes his kid will."

"Hi Matt!" Finally A.J. came running over, glove in hand. For Matthew, it was like they'd never been apart. The two boys playfully hit each other with their gloves.

"Why don't you come over tomorrow, A.J.?" Pop asked. "If that's okay with you, Donny."

"We have an extra practice tomorrow night," A.J. sighed. "Coach says we have to go back to the drawing board. Hey, maybe you can come?" A.J. turned to his friend.

Matthew looked at his grandfather.

"I'll talk to Coach Riley," Pop said. "We'll see you tomorrow."

It had been almost a week since Coach Riley reluctantly agreed to let Matthew practise with the team.

It was like old times for the boys—Matthew pitching and A.J. catching. The two boys knew each other so well they hardly had to use any signs. Just a tiny nod from A.J. and Matthew knew what to throw.

League rules didn't allow for visiting players, so Matthew had to watch games from the stands. The Beavers' losing streak was at four games now and Coach Riley was ready to quit.

After one practice, the coach pulled Matthew aside.

"I hear you may be moving back to Pembroke, kid," the big man said, leaning casually against the ballpark fence. "We sure could use your arm."

Riley scowled as he looked over to where his son was waiting for him. "That guy's a bust," he grumbled. "No matter how much we practise, he just can't do it in the games."

Matthew had noticed Tim Riley rubbing his arm several times over the last couple of practices. He wondered if the boy's father was working him too hard. But he knew better than to say anything to the coach.

"We're playing in a tournament this weekend," the Coach continued. "And I got them to agree that you can play for the team."

Coach Riley slapped Matthew on the back. "What do you say, son?"

Matthew looked nervously over at Tim. "Uh, sure," said Matthew, not at all sure.

"We'll see you then." The coach turned and glared at

his son, who meekly dropped his head and followed his father off the field.

"Did you hear that, Mr. Parker?" A.J. shouted. "We're a team again! We'll show those other Valley showoffs. They beat us all season but not this weekend."

The tournament started the next afternoon. All morning, Matthew paced around the house, feeling sick to his stomach. His mother suggested a rest in the shade—it was promising to be a scorcher.

"Is there something bothering you?" Pop asked Matthew, as he sat down on the porch swing. Matthew had been half-heartedly pushing himself back and forth, willing the knot in his stomach to go away.

"I don't know how to say it, Pop," Matthew began, reluctantly. His grandfather nodded for him to continue.

"It's Coach Riley," Matthew explained. "He's so mean to Tim. I'm just kinda scared of what he'll say if I make a mistake."

Pop shook his head and looked off into the distance.

"There are lots of people who don't remember what's really important in life," Pop said. "It's not who wins and loses."

"I know, I know," Matthew said in a defiant voice. "It's how you play the game. But what does that really mean?"

"Well," said Pop thoughtfully, "what does it mean to Jackie Robinson?"

Jackie Robinson? Matthew stared at his Pop. What did Jackie Robinson have to do with a ball game in Pembroke?

"I don't get it, Pop."

Pop didn't have a chance to explain. All at once, A.J. was running up the walk, waving his glove.

"Let's go Matt," he shouted. "I can't wait."

Matthew jumped off the swing and grabbed his glove. "See you at the ballpark, Pop."

He didn't stop long enough to see the worried look cross his grandfather's face.

A.J. was right. The Pembroke team, anchored by the two friends, was untouchable in round robin play. In one of the games, Matthew even had a no-hitter going into the fifth.

Coach Riley was sweet as honey on the bench. Tim sat at the end of the dugout, a sullen look on his face. But the rest of the boys kept slapping Matthew on the shoulder and telling him how great it was to have him back.

The final game started around four o'clock. There was not a breath of wind. The sun beat down on the players and spectators, and turned the infield dirt into dust.

Matthew was on the mound, trying to concentrate on a Renfrew batter. A.J. kept stopping to wipe his face, which was dripping with sweat behind his catcher's mask.

"Baaaaallllllll twooooo," shouted the umpire. A.J. shook his head in anger and gave Matthew another signal.

"Baaaallllllll threeeeee."

Matthew felt a surge of frustration. He was sure that had been a strike. For a moment, he wondered if the umpire was in the pocket of the other team. He'd certainly heard of such things happening, and he knew that his pitch would have been a strike in Montreal. After all, he'd watched enough big league games this season—

Suddenly, he noticed A.J. waving frantically. The umpire was rudely signalling for him to hurry up.

Matthew wound up and threw. In his haste, he sent a big, juicy fastball right across the centre of the plate. The Renfrew player didn't miss a beat. He swung the bat smoothly and surely, with a perfect follow-through. Matthew didn't even need to follow the path of the ball. He knew it was going out of the park.

A.J. came rushing up to the mound.

"What was that?" his friend yelped, a terrified look on his face.

"Have you lost your cotton-pickin' mind?" Coach Riley was so close that Matthew could see the blood vessels bulging in his neck. "If I wanted a friggin' fastball across the plate, I'd have my boy in there throwing the sucker pitches.

"Smarten up, boy," the coach muttered darkly. "Or your big-city show-off behind is out of here."

Matthew was almost shaking as he once again took his place on the mound. No adult had ever spoken to him the way the coach just had. He looked up in the stands and found his mother and grandparents. His mom's eyes met his own, and she gave him a reassuring smile. Matthew took a deep breath and turned his attention back to the game.

After five innings, the score remained the same. Matthew had struck out six of the last eight batters, but Coach Riley had not spoken a word to him since the home run.

"This is it, boys," he muttered as he walked up and down the dugout. "I spent a season being humiliated by you losers. But this is the one we are going to win."

Matthew wanted nothing more than to run out of the dugout. But A.J. was sitting beside him, almost pressing against him. He, too, seemed scared by what the coach might do next.

They were in the bottom of the sixth. Just one inning left to make things right. The Renfrew pitcher seemed distracted during Matthew's at-bat, and he was able to get on board with an easy double.

Phew, he thought. Now the coach might lay off him now.

He looked over at the dugout, expected a nod of encouragement. Instead, Coach Riley was jumping up and down, screaming about stealing bases and making a move. Matthew got into the ready position that he had learned from Jackie Robinson. As his teammate hit, Matthew dug in his feet and raced to third, even sliding in, the way they did in Montreal. The other Pembroke players cheered as he stood up and brushed himself off. He quickly smiled up at the stands and then his face was serious again.

A.J. was up at bat and the coach was yelling at him, directing him on every swing.

This is my chance, Matthew thought to himself. He gently eased himself off the base. No one on the other team even seemed to notice what he was doing. They were too busy watching A.J., his forehead sweating with every jeer from his coach.

Matthew timed his run perfectly. As the opposing pitcher pulled back his arm to release, Matthew sprang into action. He ran as fast as he could toward home plate. The Renfrew catcher was so shocked to see his opponent running toward him that he dropped the ball and froze. Matthew slid across home plate. He had tied the game!

Matthew jogged from the field into the dugout, ready to accept congratulations from his teammates for his stunning play. He couldn't wait to tell Tyrone what he had done! After all, this was something he had learned from watching Jackie Robinson.

As he stepped into the dugout, though, Matthew instantly realized something was wrong.

"What was that?" Coach Riley lunged toward him and grabbed Matthew by the front of his shirt. "Did I tell you to steal? Are you listening to me, boy?"

"You told me to steal," Matthew said, his voice constricted by the coach's grip on his uniform.

"I did not say to steal home," the coach hissed. "What kind of a foolhardy play was that? Are you in cahoots with the other team?"

"Jackie ... Robinson ... does ... it," Matthew whispered.

The coach dropped Matthew hard on the bench. For a moment, he looked as if he was going to give him a kick.

"I don't care what any nigger does," Coach Riley shouted. "This is my team. Do you hear me? My team. You ain't playin' for the goddamn Brooklyn Dodgers. And he ain't never going to neither."

Matthew sat on the bench, frozen with fear. He'd heard Tyrone and Dewey talk about people who used words like "nigger," but he'd never talked to one himself. And now, here was his coach—a racist. Matthew was too stunned to move or speak. Suddenly, his grandfather and Mr. Kirkpatrick stepped into the dugout.

"We'll take it from here, Buddy," Donny Kirkpatrick said. "All of the parents agree—you're excused from coaching duties."

Coach Riley stared at the two men. Matthew held his breath as he watched the big man, who looked as if he was about to explode. Instead, he grabbed Tim by the collar of his shirt and dragged him out of the dugout without saying a word.

"Let's finish this game off, fair and square," Mr. Kirkpatrick told the boys.

He gave Matthew a pat on the back. "Nice play, kid. I never thought I'd see a move like that here in Pembroke."

Pembroke scored another two runs against Renfrew, who seemed shocked by all that had happened. But even with the win, the post-game celebration was somewhat subdued.

"We'll talk about it all later," Pop whispered. "Try to enjoy your victory."

Matthew watched the other boys waving their trophies in the air, and he joined in as well. But still, he couldn't shake off what Coach Riley had said.

"So, Matthew, does this mean A.J. has his favourite pitcher back for good?" The boy's father walked over where Matthew and Pop were standing.

Matthew shook his head.

"I'm not staying, Coach. I'm going back to Montreal." Matthew said, trying to hide his surprise as the words poured out. "Good luck for the rest of the season."

"Thank you, Matthew," said Mr. Kirkpatrick kindly. "You're one heckuva ballplayer, and you're obviously learning a lot out there in Montreal. Maybe A.J. can come out and visit you sometime." He gave Matthew a fatherly slap on the back as he walked away.

"So you're going back?"

Matthew jumped as A.J. walked up behind him.

"I guess so," Matthew replied. "I didn't even know I was going to say that. It just came out."

"I'm not surprised," A.J. shrugged. "It sounds so great—a real big-league ballpark, friends with a famous ballplayer. Why wouldn't you want to go back?"

"Well, there's the baby," Matthew sighed. "That's going to change everything. At least here, with Pop and Grandma, I'd know that someone cared about what I was up to."

Matthew instantly felt guilty for saying something so mean about his mother and Alain. He grabbed his glove and a ball.

"C'mon, let's play catch. One last time."

The boys were quiet as they threw the ball back and forth, the summer sun slowly setting behind the ball-park. Their trophies lay in the grass, almost forgotten.

As Matthew packed that night, Pop came into his room. Matthew quickly wiped away a few tears, hoping that his grandfather hadn't seen.

"I want you to have this," Pop said, sitting down on the bed. He handed Matthew a box.

Matthew looked inside. There were a whole bunch of baseball cards and photographs. And a glove. He took it out and put it on.

"Whose glove?" he asked.

"Your father's," Pop replied softly.

Matthew touched the glove gently as his grandfather continued.

"I found this box in the attic when I was up there cleaning last month. Your uncle Stu gave it to us after your father's accident. You probably don't remember Stu. He died in the war. Your dad was quite the athlete. Reminds me of you."

"He played baseball?" Matthew asked, fingering the laces of the glove.

"Oh, yes—a pitcher, like you," Pop answered. Matthew picked up one of the photos. The yellowed edges were tattered and the grainy image looked as if it was starting to fade. But he could make out the face. And the blonde hair and freckles, bleached by the summer sun.

"You sure do look a lot like him," his grandfather said softly.

Matthew carefully took the photo and stared at it for a moment. He felt a lump in his throat. He had an envelope full of pictures of his father. He'd taken them out many times over the years. But to see a new one—taken when his father was the same age as him, playing ball ...

Matthew fought back the tears.

"You're doing the right thing," Pop said gently. "And you know you will always have a home here. But your mother needs you. And you need her. You are a family. Always were."

Matthew thought for a moment about Coach Riley and how cruel he was to his own son. And then he thought about Alain, who was so gentle, wanting nothing more than Matthew's friendship. He felt a wave of guilt as he thought about how mean he'd been to his stepfather.

"You are a lot like your father," Pop said, breaking the silence. "Colin had a big heart—and he was always looking out for the underdog. He would have been cheering for your friend Jackie Robinson, that's for sure."

Matthew smiled as he thought about his friends back in Montreal.

"I'd better finish packing," he said finally. He gently took the items his grandfather had given him and placed them in his suitcase.

"Thanks, Pop."

It was time to go home.

Chapter Ten

# Tyrone's Story

**Robinson and Teammates Brave Brawl in Baltimore**
by Dewey Barton
The pressure continues to mount on Jackie Robinson of the
Royals.

Robinson and several of his teammates were trapped by an
unruly mob after last night's game in Baltimore.

The crowd exploded after a spectacular play by Johnny
"Spider" Jorgensen. His throw from the outfield to catcher Herman
Franks ended the Orioles' chances of scoring the tying run. As
Franks reached out to tag the runner, the entire stadium erupted.

THE ROYALS WERE AWAY on a road trip when Matthew
and his mother arrived back in Montreal. Even so,
Matthew was anxious to get to the ballpark to find out
what he had missed.

He found Tyrone and René sitting in the stands—

René's rake resting in the nearby aisle—flipping through a stack of newspapers. With them was Dewey Barton.

"Yep, I was glad to get out of there in one piece," Dewey was saying as Matthew walked up.

"Welcome back, young man," Tyrone said, with a big grin. "You came back after all, even though we work you something fierce."

"I can take it," Matthew said, smiling.

"*Bienvenue, mon ami*," said René. He handed Matthew one of the papers. "*Monsieur Barton*—"

"Dewey ..."

"Dewey has brought these newspapers, all about the trip of the Royals to Baltimore," explained René.

"Poor Jackie," said Tyrone, shaking his head. "And poor Rachel. I hope she's not going to be seeing these pictures."

Matthew took the paper from Tyrone and scanned the photos in shock. Another riot in Baltimore!

"Thank goodness that was the last road trip to Baltimore. It was wild!" said Dewey. "The fans poured onto the field and then the police rolled in. Six police cars, ten officers on foot, and several boys on motorcycles."

"But this time, it wasn't Jackie's fault," the newspaper-man continued. "The mob was after the umpire this time. Said he'd cost Baltimore the game. They weren't taking any chances, though," he added. "Not after the brawl last time.

"Funny thing was, Jackie wasn't even on the field when the play happened," Dewey explained. "Jorgensen made a big play from the field, didn't even go for the cut-off man. Threw it straight all the way in to Herman Franks. What a throw!

"Trouble is, he jammed the ball right into the guy sliding into the plate and he was out," the reporter continued. "The lid came off the stadium."

"Jackie was already in the clubhouse, getting his leg fixed up." Tyrone picked up the story. "The fans started making a big ruckus outside. Jackie says it sounded like a lynch mob."

"No one knows where Clay Hopper went," Dewey added. "So three of his teammates had to stay with Jackie until the crowd finally went away."

"They stayed there until after midnight," Tyrone said with a hint of anger in his voice. "Spider Jorgensen, Rabbit Rackley, Tommy Tatum, and Jackie. They weren't sure they were going to make it out of there alive.

"Finally, some of the clubhouse attendants came back and said the coast was clear," Tyrone concluded. "They couldn't get a cab because Jackie was with them so they all ended up going by streetcar. The other fellas left Jackie a block from where he was staying.

"But Jackie never said a word through it all," Tyrone added. "The mob was yelling, 'we're going to getcha, nigger,' and Jackie didn't say a word."

Matthew looked over at the old ballplayer. He was staring out at the ball field, anger etched into his face.

"What's this article by Sam Hill all about?" Matthew asked, as he picked up another of the newspapers.

"Oh, the usual," Dewey replied. "He wants Jackie to be treated like any other player. As if that was possible! He wants Clay Hopper to yell at Jackie, just like he would at any other player. And he wants the fans to boo him if he makes a mistake. But you know that isn't going to happen."

"Unless it is Baltimore!" joked René.

Tyrone chuckled. "Jackie's getting so popular that he has Sam tag along with him after the game. If people try to give Jackie gifts, Sam tells them that Jackie could get a fine if he accepts them."

"Is that true?" asked Matthew.

Tyrone shook his head, smiling. "No, sir. But Jackie's getting worn away by all the autographs and presents. It's too much for one man."

Once again, Jackie Robinson was the only black person in the International League. This time, though, Branch Rickey had decided that Robinson didn't need another black companion. Roy Partlow had been sent down to the AA team in Trois-Rivières to join John Wright. "Jackie's still got me," Tyrone said, grinning from ear to ear.

"I heard something interesting about you on the road trip," Dewey said, looking at Tyrone. "Tell you what. I'll buy you and these boys lunch—and you can tell me whether it's true."

"Oh, I don't know, sir," Tyrone replied.

"Please Tyrone," urged Matthew, stealing a quick glance at René. He knew they were only being invited because the old man would find it harder to say no, but he didn't care. Maybe they'd finally get to the bottom of Tyrone's relationship with Jackie Robinson.

"I guess it's eating time anyway," Tyrone said reluctantly. "But I can't go to no restaurant with you. I have to eat with the coloured folks."

"Tyrone, this is Canada, remember?" replied Dewey. "You sure can come and eat with us. Let's go, fellas. I know a great joint just around the corner."

The Chic-N-Coop was a popular spot, and even the Royals players sometimes dropped by when they were in town. The walls of the restaurant were covered with black-and-white photographs of ballplayers, all autographed and neatly framed. There was a jukebox in one corner and a steady stream of the latest songs from the hit parade played in the background. Fifteen minutes after they walked in, the two boys were digging into a delicious platter of burgers and fries, with chocolate shakes on the side. Tyrone had the hot chicken sandwich, and Dewey a plate of poutine with the works. Matthew laughed as he watched Tyrone's eyes grow big as he saw the huge pile of fries and cheese curds, topped with gravy, hamburger and peas.

To Matthew, Tyrone seemed nervous. He kept glancing around, to see if anyone was looking at him. He seemed to relax as he realized that no one in the Montreal restaurant was paying any attention at all to their table.

"So, here's the story," Dewey said, taking a break from his massive plateful of poutine. "I hear that you, Tyrone, are the one who got Jackie Robinson into baseball."

The boys turned, wide-eyed, to look at their friend. His eyes were down on his food, and for a couple of seconds, he just kept eating, as if he was digesting both his food and Dewey's words.

"If I tell you ...," the old man began, putting down his fork. He picked up his napkin and carefully wiped his lips. "If I tell you, I don't want this in no newspaper. And you boys, you have to keep it to yourselves. You understand?"

"But Tyrone ...," Dewey started to argue.

"No buts," Tyrone said. "The story is Jackie Robinson—not some washed-up old pitcher from the Negro Leagues. That was yesterday's story. It never got told, mind you, but that's yesterday's news."

"Okay, okay," Dewey put away the notebook and pencil

that had been lying next to his plate. "What about when the season is over?"

"Do you want to hear the story or not?" the old man replied.

"Yes!" the two boys said together.

Tyrone paused for a moment, sighed, and then started to speak.

"It all started when Jackie was in the army," Tyrone began. "He was drafted in 1942 to go to Fort Riley in Kansas. He did his basic training and then applied for Officers' School.

"Jackie passed all the tests, but he waited for a long time to get into the school," Tyrone continued. "White soldiers who applied at the same time had already been admitted, but none of the black soldiers had been." Tyrone paused for a moment. "Have you heard of Joe Louis?"

"Of course," Matthew said instantly.

"He's the heavyweight champion of the world," said René.

"Right," Tyrone smiled. "So Joe Louis comes to Fort Riley and Jackie tells him all about what's been happening at the Officers' School. Next thing he knew, he was in, and before long, Jackie Robinson was a second lieutenant in the U.S. Army.

"Things were going smoothly until Jackie got to Fort Hood, Texas," Tyrone continued. "He got on a bus on the base and sat up front. He was told to move to the back where he belonged. You see this was in the South. Down there, my people only get to sit at the back of the bus."

"What did Jackie do?" Matthew asked, captivated.

"He stayed right where he was," Tyrone replied. "When he got off the bus, he was taken away by the military police and eventually court-martialled."

"What's a court martial?" asked René.

"It's like a trial, but for the army," replied Dewey. The newspaperman had pushed away his plate and was leaning on the table with his elbows, taking in every word of Tyrone's story.

"Jackie was declared innocent, of course," said Tyrone, his voice growing louder with anger. "He wasn't disobeying an order. This was the army! They couldn't order him to the back of the bus.

"And that's where I came into the story," he said, in a softer voice. "After the court martial, Jackie was sent to Camp Breckinridge in Kentucky to wait for his papers. He wasn't training to go overseas anymore. He wanted out of the army," Tyrone explained. "So they sent him to Breckinridge to coach some black sports teams, just until they could sort everything out.

"Jackie needed something to do next. I was working at the mess hall in them days, and we started chatting, probably about ball. I told him about my old team, the Kansas City Monarchs."

"In the Negro Leagues?" Dewey asked.

Tyrone nodded. "I told Jackie to write to the owner of the team, tell him he was interested in playing professional ball," Tyrone concluded. "He got the job."

But the story wasn't quite over.

"The war was just ending and I decided I was ready for a change of scenery," Tyrone continued. He paused for a moment to take a sip of the hot coffee the waitress had brought him.

"So I decided to pack up and head to Kansas City. Got a job working at the ball field with the Monarchs," he explained. "The owner and I had always got along well and he was even more pleased with me once he got to see Jackie play.

"That boy was a natural-born athlete," Tyrone added. "Did you know that in college he played four sports? Baseball, football, basketball, and track and field."

Dewey nodded for the old ballplayer to continue.

"Jackie didn't much like life in the Negro Leagues," Tyrone admitted. "It was a tough grind. We travelled by bus, often overnight. And when we did get hotel rooms, they were usually the worst sort, 'cause that's all the team would pay for.

"Most of the boys liked to party," Tyrone chuckled gently. "But Jackie never had time for any drinking or smoking or carrying on. And there were lots of practical jokes on the road. Jackie didn't like them much either."

Tyrone's face grew serious. "Jackie had grown up different from us in the South. He grew up in California, where folks were more accepting of blacks. I remember one time in Alabama, the bus pulled up to a filling station. Jackie asked the attendant where the washroom was."

Tyrone paused, a pained look on his face. "The man just pointed off in the distance and said, 'Your bathroom's over there.' Well, Jackie took offence right away. 'What do you mean, my bathroom?' Jackie said. And even from the bus, I could see the anger bubbling up inside him.

"And that fellow just kept at him. 'The coloured bathroom's over there and the white one's over here.'

"Before we knew it, Jackie was heading for the white bathroom. The man started yelling at him, calling him names, and Jackie hit him. Knocked him out.

"We all panicked—this was Alabama, after all. A couple of us grabbed Jackie and pushed him on to the bus. The fella was just starting to stir as we pulled him away."

Tyrone shook his head. "So I'm always worried, always watching, thinking about that day in Alabama."

Then, he smiled at the boys. "Still, we're here, right boys? All thanks to Mr. Rickey."

Tyrone took another sip of his coffee.

"I knew something was up when the Brooklyn Dodgers scouts started to come around. They told us Branch Rickey wanted to set up a new Negro Leagues team. Then he asked Jackie to meet with him."

Matthew had heard this story before, and he knew René had as well. But it was news to Dewey Barton. The young reporter had just been about to grab another forkful of poutine. Now, he stopped mid-mouthful and put his fork back down to concentrate on every word Tyrone was saying.

"Jackie came to me after the meeting, looking for my advice," said Tyrone. "'He wants me to play for his team,' Jackie said. 'For his new league,' I asked. 'No, there is no new league,' Jackie explained. 'He wants me to play for the Montreal Royals. And then to join the Dodgers.'

"It took a minute for that to sink in," Tyrone said, his eyes staring off into the distance.

Dewey's eyes were as big as saucers. Matthew thought he could see the reporter's hand twitching, he wanted so badly to be writing this story down.

"So Jackie and I headed here, to Montreal," Tyrone concluded. "I'm like a big brother to him and he looks out for me. Even now, when he's a big star."

"And you look out for him!" Matthew interjected. He thought about how gently Tyrone had encouraged Jackie when he was feeling overwhelmed, just before the game against Jersey City.

"Does that mean you'll be heading to Brooklyn, too?" asked René, taking a final sip of his chocolate shake.

"We've got to make it through this season first," the

old man chuckled.

"Thanks for the meal, kid," he said to Dewey, as he got up to head back to the ballpark. "I don't want to be reading about this in the paper, mind. At least not until the season's over."

Tyrone gave them all a big wink and headed out the door.

# Chapter Eleven

# *The Pressure Builds*

### Robinson to Remain with the Royals

by Dewey Barton

*August 28, 1946*

Jackie Robinson has had enough pressure this season, according to Mel Jones of the Brooklyn Dodgers.

Management for the Royals and the Dodgers wanted to end speculation that the Royals' hitter was headed to Brooklyn.

"He's passed the test in the International and he shouldn't have to go through all that again in the big league," Jones told reporters yesterday.

Still, this reporter believes Robinson could, indeed, crack the lineup of a big-league squad. One baseball pundit speculates that Robinson could play second base for twelve of the sixteen major league clubs.

MATTHEW HADN'T SEEN MUCH of Guy in the few weeks

since he'd gotten back from Pembroke. He had looked for him once in a while, to find out how Guy was doing. After all, he had promised to teach his new friend how to play baseball. But the other boy seemed to be spending much of his time at the factory with his mother.

When Matthew got home from the ballpark that day, he was surprised to see Guy sitting on the front step. The boy's face was pale, and his clothes were even more ragged than usual.

"*Salut*," said Matthew tentatively.

Two other boys, Guy's friends, came out of the alley just then. As soon as they saw Matthew, they started waving their sticks and yelling so fast he couldn't catch what they were saying. He just knew they were angry.

Guy got up from the step and shouted something at the boys in French. Eventually they took off back down the alley.

"What was that about?" Matthew said, his heart pounding. For a moment, he'd thought he might have to make a run for it.

Guy shrugged. "Our mothers all work in the factory together. Today, *le grand chef*—the boss—he says the factory is closing. No more jobs. He is *anglais*, and so, *mes amis*, they are angry with *les anglais* today."

"Well, your mom will just get another job, right?" Matthew asked carefully.

"Not so easy," Guy replied. "She doesn't speak English.

She can't read or write. She's worked in the same factory all her life."

"That was my future, too," Guy continued. "What will I do now? Maman, she talks about sending me back to the Townships, to live with *mes cousins*. But their house is very crowded. They have no money and no jobs. Just a farm, with too many mouths to feed."

Just then, Alain came out on the balcony to look for Matthew.

"Oh, there you are. We are having supper," he called down. "Your friend can come, too, *si tu veux*."

"Do you want to?" Matthew asked.

Guy paused. "*Oui, merci.*" He looked down at his clothes. "I am not dressed so well for supper."

"Hey, I'm covered in dirt from the ballpark," Matthew laughed. "My mom will think you look great!"

All through supper, Guy listened carefully to Matthew's stories about the latest happenings at Delorimier Downs. Matthew guessed it had probably been quite a while since Guy had a proper meal. He had several plates full of potato salad, cold chicken, and homemade biscuits. Matthew felt guilty as he thought about the enormous lunch he'd had, followed by such a plentiful supper.

He saw his mother eyeing Guy's clothes. He could hear her and Alain talking in the kitchen as they cleared the plates.

"You are very lucky to have such a good job at the ball field," said Guy, digging into a third piece of lemon meringue pie. He looked gratefully over at Grace, who gave him a warm smile.

"Well, the season will be over soon, so he'll have plenty of time for homework once school starts," his mother teased.

"Most of the staff at Delorimier, they go to work at the Forum for the winter," Matthew explained. "Maybe I could work on the weekends?"

The look on his mother's face gave him his answer. He looked over at Guy.

"I can't do it, but maybe you could!" Matthew said, suddenly excited. "Think of it! You could see every single Canadiens game. I could introduce you to Cecile—she runs the concession stands at Delorimier."

"But I don't speak such good English," Guy protested.

Matthew laughed. "I worked at Delorimier and I didn't speak a word of French! You'll be fine. We can go meet her tomorrow."

Alain returned to the table with an armload of clothes. "Now that I'm about to start teacher's college, I need some new clothes. I was just about to get rid of these. I think there may be something here in your size?"

Guy's face lit up. He seemed unable to say anything. He got up from the table and took the clothes from Alain.

"*Merci pour tout,*" he said. "*Merci, chère madame. Et mon ami, merci.*"

"Guy," Alain said, as the boy headed to the door. "If you do get work at the Forum, *est-ce que tu me promets que tu vas rester a l'école?* Please say you'll stay in school."

Guy paused. "I will try." He looked serious again. "*Merci pour tout!*"

As August drew to a close, it got busier and busier at Delorimier Downs. Some of the staff had already moved over to the Forum, so there was plenty of work to go around. Guy was an instant hit with Cecile, who hired him on the spot. Matthew made sure Tyrone had a word with her before the two boys arrived, just so things would go smoothly.

Tyrone was a little bit distant these days, spending less time at the ball field and more time at de Gaspé Street with Rachel Robinson. The old ballplayer wouldn't tell the boys exactly what was wrong, but he hinted that her pregnancy wasn't going very easily and that she had to rest as much as possible.

Jackie continued to impress on the field and so did the rest of the team. The Royals clinched their second consecutive International League title during a double-header in Rochester. Montreal now had a twenty-game lead over their closest rivals—a commanding lead with only two weeks to go in the regular season.

With the pennant a sure thing, speculation had once again started that Robinson might be called up for the rest of the season. Reporters who had initially doubted Robinson's chances to make it to the majors were now big fans. "The greatest performance being put on anywhere in sport," wrote one.

But in late August the Dodgers general manager made it official. He called reporters together and put the speculation to rest.

Matthew and René hovered behind the group of reporters at Delorimier Downs. Besides the usual crowd of Canadian writers, there were several dozen new faces. All the New York papers had come, hoping for a big announcement. Flash bulbs popped one after another as Mel Jones began to speak.

"Jackie Robinson has passed the test of the International League," said Jones, decked out in a fancy suit and leather shoes. "But he shouldn't have to go through all that again in the big league. He will spend the rest of the season here in Montreal, with the Royals. And we hope, of course, that he will bring home the championship for all the fine fans who have supported him this season."

"I don't get it," Matthew said as the boys moved back from the pack of reporters. "Jackie's obviously good enough to play in the National League. Why not call him up?"

René shrugged. "He will go next season, *oui?* Maybe it's better for him to wait until then."

"Yeah, I guess it would be kind of tough to go up there now," Matthew agreed. "Everyone on the team knows everyone else. And he wouldn't know the city or anything."

"And who knows if they would be as happy to see him as we are here in Montreal?" René added.

The boys turned back to the pack of reporters who were now shouting questions at the Dodgers general manager. He raised his hands to quiet them down.

"One question at a time, boys," Jones boomed. "And there's not much more I can tell you. It's the doctor's orders. He wants Jackie to take a break, recover for the post season. We've already clinched the pennant, so we thought it was a good idea. That's all for today."

And with that, the big man and his entourage turned abruptly and headed out of the stadium.

Dewey walked over to where Matthew and René were standing. The young reporter was still scribbling in his notebook.

"Well, isn't that the darnedest thing?" Dewey said. "Jackie's leading the league in hits, stolen bases, and fielding, and he's taking a break for five days?"

"Hope he's not just stacking his averages!" one of the other reporters said as he walked by. "The other fellas won't be too happy if it looks like Robinson is just out to win the batting title."

"Nah, Jackie wouldn't do that," Dewey said, shaking his head. "But I wonder what's up."

Two days later, four of the Royals players were called up to spend the rest of the season with the team in Brooklyn. Jackie Robinson was still absent from the ball field, following the mysterious "doctor's orders."

Matthew was finding it harder and harder to get down to the ballpark. Today, he and his mother had gone shopping for school supplies and for some new clothes for the first day at his new school.

"You know, I'm very proud of you," Grace said gently as they returned to the apartment, packages in hand. "You have done such a wonderful job of fitting in here— finding friends, learning French."

She settled on the couch and put her feet up on a stool. "I didn't realize how tough it was going to be," she continued. "Moving here to a new city, a new language. Leaving Pop and Grandma. I miss them every day."

Grace rested her hands on her growing belly and smiled over at her son. "You make it look so easy. At the store today, I couldn't figure out what they were trying to ask me. Thank goodness you were there!"

Matthew was surprised. It had never occurred to him that his mother found it hard to adjust to life in Montreal. He had just assumed that she had Alain to help her all the time.

"I'm still a little worried about school," Matthew confessed. "I mean, what if it's really hard?"

Grace smiled. "They seem very nice. And all the English kids from the neighbourhood go there. So you'll all be in the same boat. They'll make sure you keep up in French."

"But we're all going to stick out. You know, *les anglais*," Matthew fretted.

"Think about what Jackie Robinson has gone through," his mother said softly. "It's not easy being different—having a different colour of skin, or speaking a different language. But at least here in Canada, it's okay to be different."

Matthew shivered as he thought about what Jackie Robinson had gone through this season: the black cat on the field, the riots, the name calling. He realized that whatever he faced at his new school, it would be nothing compared to what Robinson had seen.

"But you'll still let me go to the ballpark, right?" Matthew asked, his eyes pleading with his mother, who burst into laughter.

"If your homework is done and your marks are good, yes, you can keep going to the ball field until the season's over," his mother replied. "How long until the playoffs begin?"

"A couple more regular season games and then the Royals will play Newark in the first series," Matthew answered. He just hoped Jackie Robinson would be back by then.

On the last weekend before school started, Matthew tried to spend as much time as he could at Delorimier Downs. He and René were there early Sunday morning, just hours before the doubleheader against Toronto. There was no one around, so they went down to the Royals' dugout and sat, soaking in the stadium from the players' point of view.

"Maman says Jackie Robinson is not injured," said René, looking over at the spot where the ballplayer usually sat. "He is ... how you say *en anglais?* His nerves are not so good."

"Alain read that in the newspaper, too," Matthew replied. "I guess that's pretty serious."

"Maman says Madame Robinson is very worried," René continued. "Jackie feels sick to his stomach and doesn't eat and doesn't sleep. That's why the doctor says he must stop playing for a while."

"I hope he's better in time for the playoffs!" Matthew said. "The Royals aren't nearly as good without him."

"Monsieur Hill is at the Robinson's to visit," said René. "And so is Tyrone. Maman says he is there often."

"Has she seen Jackie?" Matthew asked. He was so jealous that his friend lived in the same neighbourhood as the Robinsons. The French-Canadian ladies in the area all took turns keeping an eye on the pregnant Rachel Robinson. Although the women weren't able to talk much to the wife of the famous player, who spoke almost no French, they seemed to enjoy having a celebrity in their midst.

The Robinsons were now well-known around Montreal, thanks to the almost daily coverage of Jackie's exploits. Jackie and Rachel had to take two buses and a trolley to travel back and forth to Delorimier Downs. René had made the trip on the same bus as them one day, and was amazed to see how many Montrealers came up and asked the ballplayer for an autograph.

The boys stopped their conversation abruptly when they saw the familiar form of Tyrone across the field. He was carrying a bag loaded with gear.

"You boys want to do a favour for me?" Tyrone asked, as if he hadn't been away from the ballpark for a couple of weeks.

"Sure, Tyrone," Matthew replied. René nodded.

"Take this gear into the Royals' clubhouse and put it out nice and neat," Tyrone explained. "Jackie's coming back this afternoon and I have to find Mr. Hopper to let him know."

Tyrone hurried off, leaving the boys to exchange confused looks.

"That's not five days," Matthew muttered, as they lugged the heavy bag towards the locker room.

Inside, they paused for a moment to look around. Matthew had only been in the clubhouse once before and only for a few seconds.

The room had two walls filled with individual closets and shelves, one per player. At each, a full Royals uniform hung from a hook, and the shelves were filled with gloves and ball caps and shaving kits. Each player's cleats were neatly lined up at the bottom of the closet and a nameplate hung above each spot.

"Here's Jackie's," René whispered. The boys quickly got to work, carefully laying out each piece of gear to match what they saw in the other closets. Matthew saw a black-and-white photo of Rachel Robinson pinned to the wall.

She looked much younger and more relaxed in the picture than she did now. Matthew wondered if this season was proving to be hard on her as well.

As soon as they were finished, the boys hustled out of the locker room. Although they were only doing what Tyrone asked, they still didn't want to run into anyone who would tell them to get out.

As they came around the corner, the friends almost crashed into Tyrone. The old man had a worried look on his face.

"I just hope he's ready," he muttered, half to the boys and half to himself. "I told him it wasn't a bad thing to sit out a little bit longer. But he said he had to come back. The team is losing and he needs to be here."

"Is he still sick?" Matthew asked tentatively. Sometimes Tyrone was very protective of Jackie Robinson and would tell the boys to mind their own business.

"No, he's not sick no more," Tyrone said. "Now that he knows what's ailing him, he's feeling better."

The boys looked confused.

"You can't tell no one," Tyrone continued, looking around to make sure no one else was within earshot. "Jackie's been some nervous the last couple of weeks, thinking he was going to be called up to the Dodgers. Going to have to go through all that yellin' and cursin' all over again. At least here in the International League, he knows what to expect. It's gonna be okay in Buffalo, bad in Baltimore. He's come to expect that. But the Dodgers ..."

Tyrone's voice trailed off. "Now that he knows he's stayin' with the Royals, he can deal with that. So all of a sudden, he's sleepin' more, eatin' more. And he says he's got to get back, so no one thinks he's just protecting his batting average."

Matthew smiled. Like Dewey had said to that other reporter, Jackie would never do that.

"So I guess we're back in business, boys." Tyrone shuffled off down the hallway. "See you in a few hours."

# Chapter Twelve

# *Dream Postponed*

## Royals Test out Robinson at the Hot Corner

by Dewey Barton

*August 31, 1946*

With the pennant now clinched for the Royals, speculation focuses on what's next for Jackie Robinson.

Montreal split yesterday's doubleheader with Toronto. The Royals dropped the first game, 4–3, and rebounded to win the second, 10–7.

Robinson's night was not necessarily noteworthy at the plate (1-for-5 with a double and two runs). But where he played the second game did raise some eyebrows. Robinson was shifted to the hot corner, third base, where many have speculated he will play for Brooklyn next season.

The move to third follows a number of no-shows for Robinson, amidst talk that the pressure of the season had caught up with the Negro groundbreaker.

THERE WAS A TREMENDOUS CHEER from the crowd when Jackie Robinson was announced at third base. It was obvious that the fans had been following the speculation in the newspapers that Jackie was headed to the big leagues, and was being groomed for third base. The old gentleman with the white hair gave his usual battle cry: "Jackie, 'e's my boy!"

And Jackie didn't disappoint. If he felt rusty or tired after his days off, he didn't show it. In the seventh inning, Toronto had two men on base with just one out and were looking to tie up the game. Matthew put down his tray of popcorn and peanuts. He looked over at René a few sections away. His friend had done the same. The Royals fans were anxious to see how their star player would adjust to his new position. Matthew watched as Jackie slapped his glove with his hand, preparing for the next batter. For such a big man, Robinson moved with ease, and seemed constantly primed to spring into motion.

The Royals' pitcher threw a couple of balls outside. The Maple Leafs' hitter stepped into the box with a determined look on his face. He, and the crowd, knew a strike was coming soon.

Sure enough, the next pitch was a big fat strike, right over the heart of the plate. The hitter got a good rip and the ball sizzled down the third base line, right at Jackie Robinson. He caught the ball easily and fired it off to second base in one smooth motion. He made the double-play look easy, even in a position he'd never played before. A few of his teammates slapped Jackie on the back as the Royals jogged back into the dugout.

All in all, it was a good game for Jackie. He had a double, two runs, and just one error, and the Royals coasted to a comfortable 10–7 victory.

"He can play second, he can play third," Matthew said, shaking his head in amazement. "Where are they going to try him next—first?"

"I'm sure he'd be great there, too," René exclaimed as the two friends gathered up their programs and headed for the locker room.

The regular season was over. During the first week of school, Matthew pored over the sports pages, trying to figure out which awards his hero would be winning. Robinson led the league in batting average and in runs scored. He finished second in stolen bases and in field-ing percentage. And that, having missed almost thirty games due to injuries!

Robinson was modest when asked about his accom-plishments.

"I'm just happy Mr. Rickey gave me this opportunity to play with the Royals," he told reporters. "And I'd like to thank my teammates for supporting me on and off the field."

Because he was in school again, Matthew didn't have

nearly as much time to hang around the ballpark. So he was thrilled to find Dewey Barton in the stands after school on Friday afternoon. The Royals had kicked off round one of the playoffs on the previous Wednesday night, and were currently leading the series two games to none. The team had already packed up for the trip to Newark for the next three games of the series.

"I'm just trying to pick up a few more quotes before I hit the road down south for tomorrow's game," Dewey said, explaining why he wasn't with the team.

"How's school going, kid?" he asked. "I can still remember those first few days—the smell of the chalk and the sound of the pencil sharpener going non-stop! I almost miss it."

Dewey shook his head, lost in his memories for a moment. "But now I'm here, in the middle of a history lesson. Forget those old musty history textbooks! This is the real McCoy!"

He and the other sports writers were having a heyday writing about Robinson's magical season. And speculation had begun again about where Jackie would play next season—and about how he would fare if he did move up to the majors.

As always, Robinson brushed those questions aside. "The Royals are in the playoffs and that's all I'm thinking about," he said.

"You know what's funny, Matt?" Dewey said, as they

sat staring at the empty field. "Those other reporters, they all started this season calling Jackie all sorts of names. You know, 'The Coloured Comet,' 'Dark Poison,' 'Dark Danger.' It was always something about the colour of his skin.

"Now they don't call him those names anymore. They use the nickname that they've created—Robby. And 'the flashy Jackie Robinson.'

"I'm glad for that, no mistake," the young reporter continued. "But I'm just surprised they had to do it in the first place. Kind of disappointed, you know? I mean, these guys here, they were my heroes growing up. I read these boys all my life: in the *Gazette*, the *Star*. I just didn't think they'd have so much trouble accepting Jackie. That's all.

"I guess I was kind of naive," Dewey laughed. "Good old boy from Sault Ste Marie hits the big time."

"But you've got your own column now too!" Matthew exclaimed as Dewey blushed crimson.

"Not bad for a rookie, eh?" Dewey chuckled. "It's all thanks to Jackie.

"He's something else, that Jackie Robinson," Dewey said, finally, picking up his coat and camera and heading down toward the field.

"He sure is," Matthew said, with a surge of pride.

But the best was still to come.

# Chapter Thirteen

# *Battles off the Field*

## Tensions Mount as Royals Prepare to Face Colonels

by Dewey Barton

*September 27, 1946*

Montrealers who have never travelled in the southern United States may be surprised to hear of the difficulties faced by Negro fans who want to watch Jackie Robinson play in tomorrow's opening game of the Little World Series.

Blacks are welcome at Parkway Field, where the Colonels play. But they must watch from the "Jim Crow" section. And it has a limited number of seats. Already local officials are having trouble meeting the massive demand from the black community for playoff tickets. With just 466 seats, the Colonels have already had five times that many requests. However, the team is refusing to expand the Jim Crow section or allow blacks into other parts of the bleachers.

It is into this cauldron of racial tension that Jackie Robinson will step tomorrow—the first black man to play baseball in Louisville.

SEPTEMBER FLEW BY FOR MATTHEW. Life at École Pierre-Dupuy turned out to be better than he'd hoped. His class was bigger than back home in Pembroke, but he was getting to know the kids in his class, and several of them stayed after school with him, getting extra help reading and writing French. It seemed that quite a few anglophone families had moved to Montreal after the war ended. And there were many immigrants as well. There were children in his class who had moved to Canada from Eastern Europe and even Africa. Matthew no longer felt like the only one who was new to this city and this life. Best of all, the school was just a couple of blocks past the ballpark. Matthew never missed a chance to pop in at Delorimier to see what Tyrone and the others were doing.

The Royals were the talk of the school. At lunch hour, many of the boys stood around swapping baseball cards, or tossing a ball around, pretending they were their favourite Royals player. Matthew always wanted to play second base, just like Jackie Robinson.

Having handily beaten the Bears and the Syracuse Chiefs, Montreal was now headed to the Little World Series, and they were the toast of the town—even overshadowing the Canadiens, who were about to begin their season.

Alain was waiting with the newspaper when Matthew wandered into the kitchen the next Saturday morning. He waved the newspaper.

"The Louisville Colonels won the American Association title last night!" Alain exclaimed.

"Oh, the Royals are in trouble now," Matthew replied. "Louisville has a good team."

"And it's in the South," Alain said, shaking his head. "That's not going to be so easy for your Jackie Robinson."

"What do you mean?" Matthew persisted.

"Well, the president of that team, he didn't want Jackie Robinson to play in the International League," explained Alain. "There is some talk that Jackie won't be allowed to play down there."

"They can't do that!" Matthew responded. "It's the championship series!"

Alain shrugged. "We'll have to see. But even if he does play, who knows how the fans there will treat him?"

The team left that morning for Louisville and Delorimier Downs was deserted when Matthew arrived. He wandered through the empty stands, thinking about all the hours he'd spent there this summer. He smiled at the memories—meeting René, and then Tyrone, getting a job, all the great ball games. And, of course, Jackie Robinson.

"*Ton ami n'est pas ici,*" Cecile said, coming around the corner, carrying a container of popcorn boxes. "Tyrone, he went with the team to Louisville."

Matthew was surprised. Tyrone had mentioned his concern about the Colonels possibly winning the American Association. He said things would be bad for Jackie if the Royals had to play in Louisville. He even said it would make Baltimore look friendly.

"Why did Tyrone go?" Matthew asked Cecile.

She gave a wistful smile. "He didn't want Monsieur Jackie to go through it alone. He is such a gentleman, is Tyrone. *Oui?*"

Matthew smiled to himself. Cecile always got kind of gushy when she talked about Tyrone.

"Has René been here today?" he asked, getting back to why he had come.

Cecile shook her head. "I don't know where he is. He was supposed to be here on Thursday and he never showed up." She shrugged and went back to her business.

That was odd. René never missed a day of work. Matthew knew the money was important to his family. He wondered what was up with his friend. He knew that René lived in the de Gaspé neighbourhood, but he had never been to his house. He had no way to contact his friend, other than meeting up with him here.

On Sunday, Matthew walked over to the ballpark again, worried about René. The Royals wouldn't be back until the middle of the week, so the grounds crew was letting the grass grow. The cool fall weather had started, and Matthew shivered as he walked around the grassy field.

He was surprised to see René sitting alone in the Royals dugout. His friend didn't even smile as Matthew walked towards the bench. And as Matthew drew closer, he could see why. René had a black eye and a bandage on his hand!

"What happened?" Matthew asked.

"Nothing," René muttered, turning away.

"René, you can tell me," Matthew insisted.

His friend sighed. "Some boys in my neighbourhood, they beat me up. They wanted me to steal some things from here. You know, some of Jackie Robinson's things."

René shook his head sadly. "I had been bragging that I had been in the Royals' clubhouse. The boys, they didn't believe me.

"They're always picking on me, from the time I started at that school. Calling me '*indien*' et '*petit brun.*' Making fun of me all the time. So I told them I could prove it, about being in the clubhouse. That I would bring them something from Jackie Robinson's locker. But then I couldn't do it. And they beat me up."

Matthew was too stunned to answer. So this was the secret that René had been talking about! The thing that made him different.

"You didn't know, did you?" René said. "*Oui, mon père*, he was from the Mohawk people. All his family, they live on a reserve near the United States. His family won't have anything to do with *ma mère* now that my father is dead. They say he should never have married a white person."

Matthew shook his head in frustration. Why was everything so complicated? Indian people don't like white people. White people call Indian people names. White people don't like black people. The French don't like the English. It all made his head hurt.

"What are you going to do now?" Matthew asked softly.

"I can help you out." Both boys turned to see Guy standing at the doorway into the clubhouse. He was wearing his staff uniform and holding a paint brush.

"*J'ai entendu*," said Guy. "I don't like how your story ends. Those boys shouldn't have done what they did."

"We need to set this right," he concluded.

The three boys together came up with a plan. Instead of promising to bring souvenirs to the school, René would invite the boys to Delorimier Downs, supposedly to give them their pick of Jackie Robinson mementoes.

"They're so greedy, they will go for it, for sure," René said.

"It better work," Matthew added. "Because we'll be in big trouble if we get caught!"

René frowned. "I don't want to get the two of you in trouble. Especially you, Guy. You need this job."

"We're going to be careful." Guy's voice convinced

Matthew there was no use arguing. It was time to get his nerves under control and focus on the work at hand.

A few hours later, René carefully opened the door and led the two bullies into the Royals clubhouse. Matthew caught his breath as he watched them come in. He hoped René wasn't as nervous as he was.

The two boys were not much older than René. One had a pimply face and sported a tattered Montreal Canadiens jacket. The other had a brush cut and wore faded military fatigues. They spoke French slang, *joual*, that made it difficult for Matthew to follow, especially from his hiding place in the showers around the corner.

René told the boys to help themselves to the things at Jackie Robinson's locker. Matthew peeked around the corner and watched as the two descended upon the clothing like vultures. Both grabbed at a jersey and started pulling. They began shouting obscenities at each other.

Just then, Guy pushed in the locker room door, wearing a security guard's uniform. Matthew was surprised at how mature Guy looked dressed up as *le policier*. He towered over the two boys. Guy pulled them apart and threw them onto the benches.

"What's happening here?" Guy shouted in French. "You filthy thieves. You're not allowed in here. And put down all these things. I'm calling the cops."

"But it was his fault," one of the boys whined, pointing

at René. "He brought us in here."

"And why did you do that, boy?" Guy continued. "You work here, don't you? Why are you bringing low-life scum like this here to the Downs?"

"They threatened me, *monsieur*," René pleaded.

Matthew smiled at René calling Guy "*monsieur*."

"They beat me up and said they'd keep on doing it until I got them what they wanted."

"Is this true?" Guy turned to the two boys, whose faces had gone pale. Matthew could see that they had dropped the jersey and other items from the locker.

"*Oui, monsieur.* But we won't do it again!"

"And they call me names, *monsieur*," René persisted, now glaring over at the two cowering teens.

"We won't anymore, sir," the boys promised. "But please, no police. We are already in so much trouble with *le policier*."

"Well, let this be a lesson to you," Guy said sternly. "Now get out!!!"

The two boys raced out of the clubhouse. Guy went out after them and returned a few minutes later.

"They ran right out of the stadium. I followed them out to the street, just to make sure they were really gone."

"Way to go, Guy!" Matthew exclaimed.

"*Vraiment excellente!*" René echoed.

Guy beamed. "I think they will learn their lesson, no?"

The boys quickly picked up the spare gloves and jerseys

they had placed at Robinson's locker. The two boys had been so busy helping themselves that they hadn't even realized there was nothing else at any of the other players' lockers. Or that there wasn't even a name or number on the jersey.

After they were finished, René and Matthew waited for Guy, who had to return the security guard's outfit he had borrowed.

"Thanks, Matthieu," René said. "You are a good friend."

"You could have told me," Matthew said softly. "I wouldn't have cared."

His friend sighed. "I think sometimes it's easier not to talk about it. It makes my mother sad. So I don't even tell her when I get called these names.

"But I have learned a good lesson now," said René.

"How to deal with bullies?" Matthew said.

"No, from Jackie Robinson," René replied. "He can't hide that he's different. And they are so mean to him and still he doesn't give up."

"You didn't give up!"

"No, I didn't," René smiled. "Thanks to my friends."

Guy returned and the three boys walked out of the stadium.

"That felt good," said Guy. "I hate bullies. They used to pick on me at school because I was so poor. My clothes always had patches and some days I didn't have any lunch."

"But then I grew," he smiled. "And now they don't bother me.

"And," he said seriously. "I have a good life now, thanks to Matthieu and his family. I have money to help Maman—and your mother helps Maman to find work cleaning at the college where *ton père* is studying."

All three boys smiled contentedly as they walked out of the gates of the ballpark. They would be back in just over a week for the final series of the season. Only Louisville stood between them and the championship.

"Let's go for a Pepsi," said Guy. "My treat."

"Yeah, we've got a lot to celebrate," cheered Matthew.

Chapter Fourteen

# The Little World Series

## Montreal Fans Must Rally for Robinson
by Dewey Barton
*September 29, 1946*

The treatment of Jackie Robinson by the fans of the Louisville Colonels has been a disgrace.

Even my colleagues at the Louisville Courier-Journal have been compelled to apologize for the vitriol of the southern fans. Buck Carter, writing in the Courier-Journal, says, "I deplore the demonstrations of prejudice against Montreal's fine second baseman, the young Negro, Jack Robinson."

I challenge Montreal fans to come out and right the injustice that has been done to one of the greatest players this city has ever seen.

MATTHEW DIDN'T HAVE MUCH to celebrate for the first three games of the Little World Series.

On Saturday morning, just before the start of game

one, he and Alain sat anxiously by the radio, listening to the broadcasts from Louisville.

The series got off to a bumpy start when officials in Louisville turned away thousands of black fans who wanted to cheer for Jackie Robinson. The ball field's "Jim Crow" section—where black fans were allowed to sit— only held 466 people.

"Why do they call it the 'Jim Crow' section?" Matthew asked Alain during a break in the pre-game show.

"Jim Crow is a name that some white Americans used to call black people. It's not a nice name, kind of like 'nigger,' but more acceptable," Alain sighed and shook his head. "There are Jim Crow laws in some parts of the South. Those laws don't allow coloured people into theatres, or swimming pools, or even to vote."

Matthew was still thinking about Jim Crow when the announcers came back on the air. They described an amazing sight at Parkway Field. Hundreds of people were sitting on top of an old dilapidated shack next to right field. Another couple of hundred were on top of a railway building. Others were on freight cars stopped on a siding near the ballpark. One person had even climbed a telephone pole for a view of the game.

Just as the game was about to begin, a loud chorus of boos erupted from the crowd. Matthew leaned closer to the radio.

"And this boisterous crowd is letting Jackie Robinson

know what they think of his appearance here in this World Series championship game," the announcer shouted over the noise.

"It seems as if the fans also have a few choice words for Robinson," the other commentator added. "I can see some of them hanging over the edge of the fence, shouting at the Montreal second baseman."

Matthew's heart sank. Game one didn't go well. Jackie struggled at the plate and was hitless after his first two at-bats.

"C'mon Jackie," Matthew cheered as Robinson took the plate for the third time.

"That's strike one," the announcer said. "Robinson's looking tentative yet again as he sets up at the plate."

"And that's a ball—way inside. Almost looks like Jim Wilson is trying to brush Robinson off the plate."

"You'd think the boos would be enough to put Jackie off," the other commentator added. "These fans haven't let up since this game started five innings ago."

"Oh! He's been hit!" the announcer shouted. "Jim Wilson has hit Jackie Robinson on his left quadricep. That was a hard-thrown ball. Robinson is limping slightly as he heads to first."

Matthew wanted to shake the radio. And to make it even worse, he could hear the Louisville fans cheering in the background. They were so loud that the announcers couldn't continue.

Montreal went on to win game one, 7–5. But Matthew's heart ached for Jackie Robinson. The Royals' star went 0-for-5 at the plate, his worst day of the season.

Things were even tenser the next day. Game two started twenty-five minutes late after the Louisville players refused to take the field.

On the radio, the announcers speculated as to what might be behind the protest. "Could this be a backlash against the Royals' second baseman?"

It turned out, however, that Jackie Robinson was not the cause of the protest. One of the Louisville coaches had been suspended after game one for yelling at an umpire. The Colonels opted to strike until he was reinstated. With that accomplished, the game finally got underway.

Matthew grew even more discouraged for Jackie. The boos from game one continued in this outing. The second basemen had a few impressive fielding plays but went nine innings without a hit. The sports writers said the Louisville fans were throwing Robinson off his game.

"And who could blame Robinson?" Dewey had written in the Sunday morning edition of the newspaper. "It has been a long season, full of vitriol every time he headed south. To be surrounded by thousands of folks who'd just as soon lynch you as watch you play ball? That's got to wear on any man's nerves."

Matthew put down the paper in disgust. This was awful—and not at all how he'd pictured the Royals' season ending. He needed to see Tyrone, to learn how Jackie was really doing, but the old man had insisted on travelling with the Royals, even though Jackie had told him it was too dangerous. But maybe someone else at the stadium would know something. He grabbed his coat, yelled good-bye to his mom, and left.

A short while later, Matthew made his way through Delorimier's familiar passages. There were piles of boxes all around, and an unusual amount of activity as everyone got ready for the return of the Royals after Monday's game in Louisville.

Matthew was about to head up into the stands when he saw Cecile walking quickly towards him. She was holding a handkerchief and dabbing her eyes.

"Oh Matthieu, it is so terrible," she said in French, so quickly that Matthew could just barely follow. "It's Tyrone. They say he stole some money. The team, they want to send him to the police."

"But Tyrone's with the team, isn't he?" Matthew asked, his heart beating faster. "He went to Louisville."

Cecile shook her head sadly. "Monsieur Jackie, he made Tyrone come back early. He was worried there was going to be a mob and he wanted Tyrone to be safe." Cecile let out a little sob. "And now this? What will we do?"

Up ahead, they could hear loud voices. Cecile

motioned for Matthew to follow her. They came around a corner to see a pair of security guards holding Tyrone's arm. They had handcuffs on him and were moving him towards the exit.

"Wait!" Matthew said, running after them.

"Don't you worry, son," Tyrone said. "It's just a misunderstanding. We'll get it sorted out real soon."

"What did he do, *messieurs?*" Matthew asked in the best French he could muster.

"These boys turned him in," the guard replied. Matthew turned to look. Standing in the corridor were the two boys who had beaten up René. What were they doing back at the ballpark?

"Madame Cecile discovered there was money missing," the guard continued. "And these boys said they'd seen this man taking the money."

"I don't have no money on me," Tyrone protested. "But they still don't believe me."

Matthew stared over at the boys. "*Monsieur*, these boys were here before, trying to steal from the Royals clubhouse. One of the other guards, he caught them and threw them out."

"Maybe they have the money!" Cecile said, wagging her finger in their direction. "They sound like trouble-makers."

The head guard turned to his assistant. "Check them out."

"You can't do that," the boy in the Canadiens jacket squealed.

"You were trespassing," the guard said sternly. "You've already broken the law."

The burly guards approached the two boys, who exchanged worried glances. "Empty out your pockets."

All at once, the pimply-faced boy started to cry, quietly at first and then louder. His friend gave him a disgusted look as he pulled a bag out of his pocket. He tossed it to the security guard.

"Take them down to the Centre-Ville police station," the head guard said, shaking his head as the two boys were led away. He pulled a key out of his pocket and unlocked the handcuffs on Tyrone's wrists. The old man was silent as the guard carefully put the cuffs back on his belt.

"I'm sorry," the guard said in a quiet voice. "We shouldn't have been so quick to listen to those boys."

"That's right," said Cecile. "You should have listened to Tyrone. Why you would take the word of those boys over this man ..."

Tyrone shook his head and Cecile stopped mid-sentence.

"I'm going to go get cleaned up," he said softly. "We've got lots to do before the team gets back."

The old man started to leave, but then turned back. "And thanks, Matthew. Thanks for believing me."

Matthew watched as Tyrone walked away, limping

slightly but with his head held high.

The security guard muttered another apology to Cecile and headed toward the exit.

Cecile startled Matthew by pulling him close to her into a giant bear hug. "*Merci encore*," she said as she hurried away to check on Tyrone.

When Matthew got home, he told his mother and Alain what had happened.

"What a shame," his mother said. "Even after everything that Jackie Robinson has done, that something like that could happen."

"You think it was because he's Negro that the guards didn't believe him?" Matthew asked. "That just seems so mean."

Alain shrugged his shoulders. "You'd think in Montreal, in Canada, such a thing could not happen. But it does."

"Does that mean we're no better than the United States?" Matthew said, disappointed.

"Oh no," Grace replied, sensing his concern. "After all, Jackie Robinson is able to live and play baseball here in Canada. It just means that we all still have a long way to go before everyone believes that everyone is equal."

"I thought Jackie had proved that," Matthew shook his head in frustration.

"One man can't do it all," Alain replied. "Change takes time. Jackie Robinson has done a great thing. But there will be more challenges to come."

"And you did a great thing, too, standing up for Tyrone," his mother said proudly.

"I guess so," Matthew sighed. He wished the whole thing had never happened. Even if those boys had been caught, it didn't make right what had happened to Tyrone.

On Monday, things continued to go badly for the Montreal Royals in Louisville. Matthew wondered what it was like for Jackie Robinson to have most of the crowd rooting against him.

Jackie finally got a hit in the third game, but he just wasn't himself at the plate. According to Dewey, though, Robinson had still made some incredible plays against the Colonels.

"The superb second baseman for the Royals put on a fielding display that should have quieted the discontented Louisville fans," wrote the young newspaperman. "Robinson's arm was in tip-top shape throughout the series down South. If not for his defence, the two losses would have been even more sizeable. No doubt the talented second baseman can't wait to get back north of the border, where the Royals fans appreciate his talent."

The Royals had lost two of the three games in Louisville, and in Montreal, hopes for the world championship were fading fast.

Matthew had hardly been able to concentrate on

school all week. And he wasn't alone. Every one of his classmates had stayed up late listening to the Royals' games on the radio and many were bleary-eyed the next day in class.

Now, however, the first home game was just a day away. On the playground Tuesday afternoon, Matthew was surprised to hear a group of boys bragging about having tickets to the Royals' game.

"It's a sellout, you know," one of the boys said haughtily.

"My dad is taking me, too," said another. "He says this is going to be one for the history books."

"Yeah, my dad's a big sports fan too," the other replied. "He wouldn't miss this for the world. He says no real sports fan would."

That night, Matthew kept thinking over what the boys had said. He thought about all the time he and Alain had spent talking about Jackie Robinson.

Oh well, he shrugged. If it was a sellout, there was nothing he could do. He turned off his light and fell into a restless sleep, his dreams haunted by boos.

When Matthew woke up Wednesday morning, he couldn't believe his eyes. The entire city was covered in snow.

He went running out to the kitchen. "Snow!" he shouted.

His mother laughed. "Yes, we noticed, Matthew."

"Seven inches of it, they say on the radio," Alain added. "That's going to make for some game."

"I'd better get going," Matthew said, grabbing a piece of toast from the table. "They're going to need all of us down there, clearing off the field."

"I'll give you a ride over there," Alain said, kindly. "Maybe they could use another set of hands. I have the day off. I'd be happy to help out."

"Uh, no, that's okay," Matthew replied awkwardly, trying not to look down at his stepfather's artificial foot. "There's not going to be any place to park," he added, wondering if that sounded like a stupid excuse. "It's better if I walk."

"Well then, I guess you're headed to school," his mother said sternly.

Matthew sighed. "What about after school?"

He watched as his mother turned to Alain. "What do you think?"

Matthew held his breath. He'd been so awful to Alain. Why would his stepfather help him now?

"I can drive you down there," Alain said kindly. "And don't worry; I won't stay."

"Thanks," Matthew muttered, rushing out of the room to get changed for school. He was thrilled to be heading to the ballpark after school, but somehow, he felt worse than ever about Alain.

There was no time to run home for supper after school, so Alain gave him some money. Matthew grabbed a hot dog and sat down in the stands to eat before the fans arrived. René went to get a couple of Pepsis and fries.

Many of the ballplayers had started to arrive. A few of them came out to the field to check out the snowy surroundings.

"It's him!" gasped Matthew, as he saw a tall figure walk out of the dugout and onto the field. He'd recognize Jackie Robinson anywhere. He wondered where René was. He didn't want to miss this.

Matthew stood up in the stands for a closer look. He saw Robinson walk up to home plate and stand there for a moment. Then, he slowly did a circle, looking up to the far reaches of the stadium. As he did, his eyes landed on Matthew, anxiously watching him.

Matthew caught his breath as Jackie Robinson gave him a smile and a quick wave. Then he turned and walked back into the dugout.

It had only been a moment but Matthew was thrilled to have made contact with the player he had watched all summer. When René returned, he didn't tell him what he had seen. This was something he wanted to keep all to himself.

Soon, the Montreal fans were packed into the stadium, roundly booing the Colonels as they came out onto the field. And they kept it up, too, booing every time a

Louisville player came to the plate. It was revenge, Matthew guessed, for what Jackie Robinson had gone through down South.

With their fans rallying behind them, the Royals staged a come-from-behind victory. The Colonels had a 5–3 lead into the bottom of the ninth, but Louisville starter Otey Clark gave up a walk with the bases loaded. Jackie Robinson drove home the winning run.

The next day was just as exciting. By the fifth inning of the fourth game of the series, things were looking bleak as the Colonels took a commanding 4–0 lead. But the Royals, buoyed by their fans, battled back.

"C'mon Jackie," Matthew whispered as the second baseman came up to the plate.

The Louisville pitcher had been struggling, and two potential runs were on base.

Strike one. Robinson had taken a big swing, anxious to get on base.

Then it was the pitcher's turn to show his nerves. He threw three balls in a row, putting the count in Robinson's favour.

"Count is three and one," yelled the ump.

In the stands, Matthew stood stock still, a bag of popcorn clutched in his hand.

"That's it, Jackie," he mumbled. "Patience. Wait for your pitch. It's coming ..."

And there it was: a juicy fastball on the left-hand corner of the plate. The muscular ballplayer swung the bat hard, sending the ball deep to left field. He quickly rounded first and settled at second base. The Royals runner scored as the crowd cheered.

The Montreal fans knew what was coming next. Jackie danced his way off second base as the Colonels pitcher nervously checked over his shoulder. He kept looking from Robinson to the batter, until finally he threw.

With a powerful surge, Robinson roared toward third! The catcher didn't even bother to throw. Robinson was safe, and in position to score the third run. All around Matthew, the Montreal fans were on their feet.

There was a loud crack of the bat as the next Royals player connected with the first pitch.

"Yes! Yes! Yes!" Matthew cheered as Jackie Robinson scored easily.

"You don't get much more exciting than this, boys!" Dewey Barton had come down to stand next to Matthew. A moment later, René also appeared.

By the bottom of the sixth, Louisville had a 5–3 lead. Matthew and René put down their peanuts and popcorn and found a spot down near the field to watch the end of the game. The fans were too busy cheering to buy anything.

Dewey had his notebook out and was madly jotting down notes.

"It's going to be a crackerjack finish!" he said in an excited voice.

The tension mounted in the next two innings, with the Royals batters all over the Louisville pitchers. Now, it was their last chance at the plate, time to do or die.

Marv Rackley came up to bat, with Montreal runners on second and third.

"They're going to walk him," Dewey said, shaking his head in disbelief. "And look who's up next?"

There was Jackie Robinson in the on-deck circle, swinging his bat back and forth, oblivious to the roars from the crowd as Rackley took first base.

Now, the bases were loaded for Montreal. Robinson walked up to the plate. He swung his bat gently, bent his knees a few times and took his usual stance. Matthew held his breath.

"What a great story this would be," whispered Dewey.

Matthew nodded, fingers crossed, willing Jackie to hit the ball.

He watched in amazement as the big man surprised everyone in the ballpark with a squeeze bunt that scored Al Campanis from third as the crowd erupted. It was a daring play, one that no one expected and it was all the Royals needed!

"They're back in it now," Matthew said, as he and René wound their way through the crowd. But could the Royals really come back and win the Series?

# Chapter Fifteen

## *Il a Gagné ses Epaulettes*

### Royals Rally in Game Five

by Dewey Barton

*October 3, 1946*

Faster than you can say Jackie Robinson, the Royals have gone from underdogs to favourites in the Little World Series!

Last night, Robinson rallied his team with a daring bunt. It caught everyone by surprise, most of all the fielding staff for the Colonels, to carry his Royals to victory.

The Royals are now just one win away from being crowned World Champions.

THE NEXT DAY, the entire city was buzzing with news of the comeback win by the Royals. Matthew couldn't believe it. After coming home from Louisville down two games to one, the Royals had fought their way back.

Montreal now had a 3–2 lead in the Series, and were

just one win away from being crowned world champions.

The sixth game was a Friday night, and at breakfast, Matthew had pleaded with his mother to let him go.

"I promised Cecile I would be there," he insisted. "My marks are good," he persisted. "You said I could go if I worked hard."

"No," his mother replied firmly, settling uncomfortably on the couch. Grace was now almost eight months pregnant and tired easily. "I don't want you out that late on your own. There have been warnings in the newspaper about what could happen tonight if the Royals win," his mother continued. "It's no place for a twelve-year-old boy. And that's final."

Matthew knew he had only one choice.

"What about Alain? He could take me and pick me up," Matthew suggested.

His mother looked disappointed. "You know Matthew, sometimes you are very selfish. Alain offered to take you to the ballpark the other day and you didn't want him to. In fact, you hurt his feelings."

"But he couldn't have helped. You know, with his foot—" His mother's face made him stop in mid-sentence.

"Now, when you need him," she continued forcefully. "You think you can just turn around and ask him to do your bidding. Well, it doesn't work that way."

"What doesn't work that way?" Alain was just walking in the door.

"Nothing," Matthew muttered and ran to his room.

He picked up his glove and threw it at the Royals poster on his wall. He couldn't believe it. He was going to miss the most important game of the season, possibly the last game of the season! It wasn't fair. They couldn't do this to him.

Later, when he returned from school, Matthew was surprised to see Guy waiting on the step for him. Guy had on his uniform already, even though the game was still three hours away.

"They want us down there as soon as possible," Guy said. "I'll walk over with you if you're ready to go."

"I can't," Matthew said sourly. "THEY won't let me." He rolled his eyes upward, toward his family's apartment.

"But maybe I should," he said suddenly. "Yeah, let's go."

Guy grabbed his friend's arm. "Matthieu, you can't disobey your parents."

"You have no idea what it's like," Matthew fired back. "Your maman treats you like an adult. You're allowed to do whatever you want. You're not treated like a baby."

Guy shook his head. "I wish I had parents like yours. They don't treat you like a baby. They just look out for you. My maman never has time to do that for me."

"They're not my parents," Matthew replied in a nasty voice. "He's my stepfather."

Guy shrugged. "I've got to go."

"I'll see you down there," Matthew said and ran up the stairs as his friend headed up the street.

Matthew turned the key quietly in the lock and went into the apartment. He looked over at the kitchen table where there was a plate of food, a glass, and a note. The note was from his mother: *"I've gone to my doctor's appointment and will be home by suppertime. Help yourself to a snack. Love, Mom."*

Matthew put down his school bag and stared at the note. If she wasn't going to be home until suppertime, it would be too late to convince her to let him go to the ballpark. He grabbed the sandwich off the plate and headed for the door.

As he walked toward Delorimier Downs, Matthew tried not to think about what he was doing, but instead concentrated on the game ahead. If the Royals won, they would be world champions. If they lost, they'd head back to Louisville for the seventh and deciding game. None of the Montreal players wanted to do that, especially Jackie Robinson.

When he got down to the ballpark, he went to the locker room and quickly put on his uniform. René came in just as he was finishing up.

"You're here!" René said, surprised. "Guy said your parents said you couldn't come."

"They changed their minds," Matthew mumbled,

embarrassed he had to lie to his best friend.

"You're lucky," said René. "Because this is going to be great! Aren't you excited?"

"Uh, yeah," Matthew replied, his stomach churning. "I have to go find Tyrone."

Matthew charged out of the change room and down the hallway. He heard Tyrone's voice and headed to find him. He rushed around the corner and almost crashed into Tyrone, who was deep in conversation with someone.

Matthew froze in his tracks. It was Jackie Robinson.

"Hey son, I thought you couldn't make it tonight," Tyrone said kindly. "It's good to see you, boy."

Matthew couldn't speak. He just stared at the famous ballplayer.

"You know Jackie Robinson, I believe," said Tyrone, chuckling. "Jackie, this is Matthew Parker. He's the one who helped me out in that situation I told you about."

"Pleased to meet you, Matthew," Jackie said, reaching out his hand. Matthew shook it, startled by the ballplayer's firm grip. Jackie towered above him, but looked down at Matthew with a kindly grin.

"I appreciate what you did for my friend Tyrone," Jackie said gently. "You set things right and that makes you a good man in my books."

Matthew continued to stare. He wanted to say something but it was as if his mouth wouldn't move.

"Well, I better get going, Ty," said Jackie, turning to

the clubhouse.

Then the ballplayer paused and turned back to Matthew.

"And why were you going to miss this game?" he asked Matthew. "You've been here all season, haven't you?"

"Well, my mom was worried and said I couldn't come out here alone," Matthew mumbled. "And I was mean to my stepfather. Um, my dad. So I couldn't ask him. And now I snuck down here—"

Matthew suddenly realized he was babbling.

Jackie gave him a gentle smile. "You know, I'm going to be a dad someday soon. You have to treat your father with respect. But I think you've learned that now, haven't you?"

Matthew nodded his head sadly.

"Tyrone, can we help this boy out?" Jackie asked, turning to his old friend with a playful smile. Tyrone nodded and smiled back. Matthew was about to ask what he was talking about, but Tyrone's expression changed, becoming serious again.

"And what about you?" Tyrone said, looking Jackie straight in the eye.

"I'll be fine," the ballplayer told the old man, giving him a gentle tap on the arm. "We've made it this far, haven't we?"

And with a wink at Matthew, Jackie Robinson disappeared into the club house.

Tyrone turned to Matthew. "Well, how are we going to sort out your mess, boy?"

"I think I have an idea!" Matthew said, in an excited voice. And the two of them took off down the hallway.

Thirty minutes later, Matthew raced up the stairs of the apartment block, and almost collided with Alain.

"Where are you going in such a hurry?" Alain asked, resting on the railing. He raised his eyebrow when he realized Matthew was wearing his uniform.

"I'm coming to get you," Matthew said, struggling to catch his breath. He had run all the way from Delorimier Downs.

"To get me?" Alain asked. "I was just coming down to the ballpark to get you."

Matthew could feel his face getting red.

"I wanted to find you before your mother realized what you had done," Alain explained. "I left her a note saying we were both going to see the game."

"But you didn't have ..." Matthew started.

Alain waved his hands to stop him.

"I know, I didn't have a ticket. But I was going to wait for you after the game to make sure you got home safely."

Now Matthew felt doubly bad. He had been so mean to Alain and yet his stepfather was prepared to do all this for him. Suddenly, Matthew's face brightened.

"But you do have a ticket! I got one. From Jackie Robinson!"

"What?" Alain's mouth hung open as he stared at the ticket in Matthew's hand.

"I'll tell you on the way," Matthew said, heading down the stairs. "We don't want to be late."

The game was everything Matthew dreamed it would be. He made sure he was assigned to work in Alain's section and every time he walked by, he gave his stepfather a smile or a wave.

Delorimier Downs was packed tighter than Matthew had ever seen it. He wasn't sure how they'd squeezed in so many people. Fans were standing and sitting everywhere, even on the cold cement steps. But no one was complaining.

And the Royals didn't disappoint. Pitcher Curt Davis was brilliant, shutting down the Colonel bats, inning after inning.

Unfortunately, the Louisville pitcher was also having a good game. He held off the Royals until the third.

"Phew," Matthew said to Alain, watching Jackie round first after a solid line drive. "I thought they were never going to get a hit."

"Don't worry," said Alain with a smile. "There's still a lot of ball game left." There was a cheer as Jackie raced for second, and then third. A triple!

With his teammate in a position to score, Al Campanis laid down a perfect squeeze bunt. Everyone in the crowd leapt to their feet as Jackie Robinson crossed home plate. Royals, 1; Louisville, 0.

In the next inning, however, the Colonels came on strong. Most of the fans were too caught up in the action to want anything from the vendors. Matthew leaned against a wall, close to the section where Alain was sitting. He was so intent on watching the game that he hardly noticed that Tyrone had come up beside him.

"They're not giving up," said Tyrone, pausing for a moment to catch his breath. "Jackie's gotta be sharp now."

It was as if Jackie heard him. On the very next play, he threw himself behind second, scooping up a sharply hit ball and then scrambling to the base. As if that wasn't enough, Robinson then hurled the ball to first. A picture-perfect double play.

"That's my boy," said Tyrone proudly, giving a hearty laugh. "I taught him everything I know." The old man was still chuckling to himself as he headed back into the underbelly of the stadium.

Jackie had a hit in the fifth, but the Royals were themselves the victims of a stellar double play. The two teams exchanged hits in the sixth, but it was still 1–0 heading into the seventh.

"We're supposed to stop selling in the ninth," advised

Guy, who was going around to all the young vendors. "Cecile wants to make sure no one gets hurt when the Royals win. She says everyone will pour onto the field. I can't believe I'm here," Guy added, smiling at Matthew. "I never knew baseball could be so exciting."

"Now all you hockey fans know what you've been missing," Matthew teased.

They were interrupted by a cheer. The Royals had a man in scoring position, thanks to another hit from Jackie.

On the next play, a line drive by Al Campanis drove in the runner. Montreal now had a 2–0 lead, and the crowd went wild.

"It's still not enough," Matthew muttered to himself. He and René met in the locker room at the end of the eighth and quickly changed out of their uniforms. They went to sit on the steps next to Alain to watch the end of the game.

It was now the top of the ninth, and the Royals were three outs away from clinching the victory and the Little World Series. But their nerves were getting the better of them. A poor throw to first was followed by a solid single, and quickly, the Colonels had two men on with no outs. Matthew buried his face in his hands, afraid to watch.

"They can do it!" Alain patted Matthew on the shoulder. He held his hands over his eyes, sneaking peeks now and then through his fingers. The crowd was raucous, still booing every Colonels player who came to the plate.

Matthew heard the crack of the bat and dropped his hands from his face. Jackie Robinson sprinted over to a ball that had dropped a few feet in front of him. He scooped it up handily and scrambled back to tag second before completing the throw to first.

To Matthew, it looked as if the batter had crossed first after the Royals first baseman had the ball, but it was too hard to tell. For a moment, the stadium was quiet, waiting for the decision. Then, a huge cheer went up in the stands. It was another double play, thanks to Jackie Robinson.

With that, the wind seemed to go out of the Louisville sails. The next Colonels batter took a big swing and missed for strike one. Then Curt Davis dug in his heels. It was strike two on a called strike. Only one more strike needed to end the game—and the Series.

Davis wound and threw, and the batter connected. It was a pop-up, just in front of home plate. The catcher, Herman Franks, raised his glove and the ball dropped neatly in. The batter was out and the game was over.

The crowd screamed with joy as they pushed their way out of the stands and poured onto the field. Matthew was swept into the crush and moved onto the grass. Just ahead, he could see several of the Royals trying to help Jackie Robinson through the swarm of cheering fans. Finally, they were able to get him to the clubhouse.

"Matthew!" Alain shouted. Matthew squeezed his way over to where his stepfather was standing.

"I almost lost my foot, everyone was moving so fast!" Alain said, laughing at himself. Matthew grinned.

"I'm glad you were here," he said, hoping his stepfather could hear him over the cheering.

"Me too," Alain replied. Just then, the crowd started singing.

"*Il a gagné ses épaulettes.*"

"What does that mean?" Matthew asked.

"It's an old French expression that means he has earned his wings. Actually '*épaulettes*' means 'shoulder pads,' but that doesn't make much sense in English, does it?" Alain laughed.

"It's like the song you sing ... what is it? 'For He's a Jolly Good Fellow!'" Alain continued. "I learned that one during the war."

There was an enormous cheer as Jackie Robinson stepped out of the Royals clubhouse and was instantly swept onto the shoulders of some burly fans. He was wearing street clothes now, and some women grabbed him and kissed him as he went by. Others pulled on his pant legs and reached up to shake his hand.

"Look," said Alain. "He has tears in his eyes."

As he watched, Matthew could feel his own eyes welling up with tears. What a moment. He looked around for Tyrone. He could only imagine how the old man's heart was swelling with pride now.

The crowd carried Jackie Robinson back to the dugout, where some of the Royals staff helped guide him back into the clubhouse. There was another loud cheer as he disappeared from sight.

"Doesn't look like they're going anywhere soon!" a familiar voice said from behind Matthew and Alain.

"You must be Alain," Tyrone said, as he reached out his hand.

"And you must be Tyrone," Alain replied, giving him a hearty shake. "We've heard all about you this summer."

"And what did you think of the game? Glad you were able to make it, I'd bet!" Tyrone gave Matthew a big wink.

"I can't believe it's over," Matthew said, scanning the crowd for any signs of Jackie Robinson.

"Oh, it's not over," Tyrone said. "This is just the beginning."

"What will he do now?" Alain asked.

"Well, he's got some fool notion that he wants to barnstorm across the United States for a few months," answered Tyrone. "He's talked lots of the boys into joining him, mostly coloured boys. But I hear Al Campanis and Marvin Rackley are game to go along.

"And then he's been asked to play for a few games with the Los Angeles Red Devils," Tyrone continued. "A basketball team, if you can believe it!" The old man just shook his head, but he had a smile on his face.

"Will he ever come back to Montreal?" asked Matthew.

Tyrone gave him a kind smile. "We all had a wonderful time here in your city, son. But I'm thinking Jackie's going to be living in Brooklyn next spring. At least that's what I'm hoping for."

"Has anyone told him that?" asked Alain eagerly.

Tyrone shrugged. "Not in so many words. But the deal with Mr. Rickey was one year in Montreal, then up to Brooklyn. I believe he's a man of his word. At least he has been so far."

There was another cheer as Jackie headed out the door again, this time carrying a bagload of gear.

"I'd best be getting in there to help him," Tyrone said, turning to make his way through the crowd. "You keep working on that pitch of yours, Matthew. You could be in the big leagues someday too."

And with that, Tyrone took a ball out of his pocket and placed it in Matthew's hands. Then, he disappeared into the crowd.

Matthew looked down at the baseball. Right across the seams was a signature. "To Matthew, From Jackie Robinson."

Alain and Matthew watched as the fans followed Jackie Robinson out of the stadium, still cheering loudly. Matthew wanted to run after them and yell "thank you," but he knew Alain could never keep up. And right now, he couldn't wait to get home and tell his mother about their adventures.

"Let's go home," said Matthew shyly. "Mom is going to be amazed, isn't she?"

Alain put his arm around Matthew's shoulders and gave him a gentle smile. "Yes, she will."

In the newspaper the next day, Dewey Barton reported that the crowd chased Jackie through the streets of Montreal for several blocks before a private car stopped and whisked him away.

"As one of my fellow reporters said to me," wrote Barton. "It was probably the only day in history that a black man ran from a white mob with love instead of lynching on its mind."

He ended his article: "Here's to you, Jackie Robinson."

## Chapter Sixteen

# *One More Tryout*

**Is Jackie headed to Brooklyn? Speculation Continues**
by Dewey Barton
*March 30, 1947*

Here at spring training, a buzz continues to build around the future of Jackie Robinson. The Montreal Royals star addressed the question during a brief time out at spring training yesterday.

"I got along fine in Montreal," Robinson told reporters. "I made friends there. The team, I am sure, did not suffer by my presence. We won the pennant by as big a margin as we pleased and went on to win the Little World Series.

"That couldn't have happened if Montreal's morale was not as high as it should be," he declared. "No sir, morale is mighty important."

BY THE NEXT SPRING, Matthew had a new baby in his family. Jack, they called him, much to the delight of his older brother.

With school in full swing and baseball not yet started, Matthew didn't see much of René, but he got updates every once in a while from Guy, who was thriving in his job at the Forum.

"Those boys—those bullies," said Guy. "They stay far away from René now. He's doing well at school, *oui*. And he talks about playing for *les Canadiens* when he grows up."

"*Les Canadiens!*" Matthew laughed. "Whatever happened to playing for the Royals?"

"I guess it depends what time of the year it is," Guy chuckled. "He's a boy for hockey these days. But I'm sure this summer, he will have baseball on the mind again."

No one had seen Tyrone since that final game. He had left Montreal shortly afterward with the Robinsons, bound for California.

"Cecile, she says her heart is broken," says Guy, fluttering his eyelashes, imitating their boss. "I say, *mais*, he could come back. And she says, no. Jackie Robinson won't be back."

Matthew continued to follow Jackie Robinson's career faithfully, reading everything he could lay his hands on. The first edition of *Sporting News* for 1947 had had a full page about Jackie Robinson's prospects in the season ahead. Two veteran writers vehemently disagreed over whether or not Robinson would make it in the major leagues.

In February, though, Robinson's hopes had seemed to suffer a setback. His name was not included in the Brooklyn roster for the next season.

"How could that be?" Matthew asked at breakfast one morning. "Does that mean he's coming back here?"

Alain shook his head. "No. The Dodgers are saying that he just isn't eligible for the major league draft. So if they leave him on the Montreal roster, they can protect one of their other players in Brooklyn."

"So when does he get to join the Dodgers?" Matthew persisted.

"Hmmmm," Alain said, skimming the article further. "Ah. It says he can't join the Dodgers until spring training.

"We'll know more then," he concluded.

Matthew was relieved. As much as he would love to see the ballplayer spend another season with the Royals, he also knew that Jackie Robinson deserved to be in the major leagues.


Now it was spring, almost a year after the first time Matthew visited Delorimier Downs. As he walked the now familiar streets of his neighbourhood, he smiled as he remembered how excited he had felt that day—when he'd first heard the noise from the stadium and discovered the place that would become his second home.

He thought, too, of the first time he saw Jackie Robinson. The tall, broad-shouldered man carried a heavy burden that summer of 1946. Matthew frowned as he remembered the riots in some of the American cities that Jackie visited, and the black cat in Syracuse.

Matthew felt the sun warm on his face and thought of Jackie Robinson, now down in Cuba, at spring training with the Royals. The newspaper reports said it hadn't been easy. Branch Rickey had moved the Dodgers' camp to the Hispanic country, hoping to avoid the racist incidents that Jackie had suffered at his first spring training in Florida.

Even so, things hadn't gone smoothly. There were four black players assigned to the Royals this year, along with Jackie Robinson. While the Dodgers stayed at the luxurious Hotel Nacional, and the white Royals at a posh military academy, Robinson and his black teammates stayed at a musty third-rate motel. None of them spoke any Spanish, and Jackie ended up getting sick from the Cuban food. And there was still no word when, or if, he would be called up. Worst of all, the Dodgers management had decided Robinson would try out for the team at first base, a position he'd never played.

The reporters following the Dodgers also had a field day when they got hold of a petition being circulated by the players, against Jackie Robinson. Then somebody leaked the story of a midnight meeting between the players and manager Leo Durocher. He was quoted as saying, "I don't care if a guy is yellow or black, or if he has stripes like a zebra, I'm the manager of this team and I say he plays." Durocher threatened to trade anyone who continued to resist Robinson's presence on the team. Two players eventually asked to be traded and were.

Spring training had turned around for Robinson when the teams went on a road trip to Panama. It was there that Robinson played against the Dodgers for the first time. He'd had hit after hit off the Brooklyn pitchers, and ended up the series with the highest batting average of any Brooklyn or Montreal player.

Just when it looked as if Robinson was about to make the major league team, his stomach problems returned. The Royals manager switched him back and forth between first and second base, and Jackie made several fielding mistakes. He also collided with the Brooklyn catcher, injuring his back. Jackie was unable to play in the rest of the games in Cuba. And so, Robinson finished spring training just as he had started: as a member of the Montreal Royals.

Matthew was outside the gates of Delorimier Downs now. The Royals were in New York for one final series against the Dodgers, and most of the staff was still working at the Forum. The place was almost deserted. He walked the empty hallways, wishing he'd had a chance to say a proper goodbye to Tyrone. Matthew knew Tyrone would be following Jackie Robinson. He wondered if the old player had even gotten to go to Cuba with Jackie. Matthew grinned at the thought of Tyrone walking on a sandy beach.

Matthew made his way through the gates and into the stands. The field seemed so bright and green now, compared to those cold, snowy championship games last fall. He smiled as he recalled the last game of the season, when the Montreal fans had lifted Jackie Robinson on their shoulders and sang for his victory.

"Hey, kid!" Matthew jumped as he heard a familiar voice. It was Dewey Barton, running down the steps, two at a time.

"Hey kid, did you hear the news? He made it! Jackie Robinson is a Brooklyn Dodger!"

Matthew stared at the young reporter, too surprised to speak. Dewey flopped down in the seat beside him, breathing heavily from his trip down the stairs.

"I'm here looking for some reaction," the reporter explained. "It happened this afternoon in Brooklyn. I was listening to the game on the radio.

"You know, Sam Hill has been saying for a week now that Jackie was going to be called up on April 10," Dewey said, grinning. "This was the last time the Royals would be playing the Dodgers. Perfect timing! Sam sure was right on!"

"It was the sixth inning and Jackie was up to bat. The Dodgers went up to the press box and handed out the release. It was just two sentences." Dewey smiled as he pulled a piece of paper out of his pocket. "'The Brooklyn Dodgers today purchased the contract of Jack Roosevelt Robinson from the Montreal Royals. He will report immediately.'"

Dewey chuckled again. "Jackie didn't know what was going on. He bunts into a double play and his teammates cheer. See, the Royals had heard the news on the bench, so they were cheering for him making the Dodgers, not for getting beat at first.

"After the game, he headed to the Dodgers' dressing room," Dewey continued. "They gave him a uniform with the number 42 on it. The photos will be all over the papers tomorrow."

Matthew sighed. "So he's not coming back. I guess I always knew that, but kind of didn't want to admit it.

"I'm going to miss him," he continued quietly. "I mean, I didn't really know him. But he sure was impressive to watch."

"I know what you mean, kid," Dewey nodded. "It's something to watch someone go through what he did, and handle it with such class. Even if he did have a few cases of nerves along the way, he kept going. He never fought back when they called him all those names. He had just one thing on his mind: making it to the major leagues."

"How do you think he'll do?" Matthew asked.

"Oh, I think our Jackie will do just fine," Dewey replied, smiling. "Yep, he'll be just fine."

# Epilogue

## APRIL 15, 2007

Jackie Robinson did more than just fine. He made his major-league debut with the Brooklyn Dodgers on April 15, 1947, playing first base. That first season, he was rookie of the year—an honour that now bears his name: the Jackie Robinson Rookie of the Year Award.

Robinson had his most brilliant season in 1949. He was thirty years old then, and led the league in batting and stolen bases. Robinson was named most valuable player that season, just two years after making his major-league debut.

He finally won the World Series in 1955 and quit a year later, after being traded over the winter to the Giants. He was inducted into the Baseball Hall of Fame on July 23, 1962, the first African-American to achieve that honour.

Jackie Robinson died in 1972, at the age of 53.

I never saw Jackie Robinson again after that amazing summer of 1946, other than on the television and movie screen. And I don't know what happened to Tyrone. Dewey went to New York a couple of times and tried to ask around, but he never did find out what happened to the old ballplayer.

I played ball in high school and even got a scholarship to a U.S. college. But I hurt my throwing arm in my senior year, and had to give it up. I came back to Montreal and got a job, met my wife, and settled down to have a family.

These days, I throw the ball around with my grandson, named Jackie. Sometimes, I take him to the spot where Delorimier Downs used to stand and tell him about my front row seat for a piece of baseball history. There's a statue of Jackie Robinson, up near the Big O, where the Expos used to play. Unfortunately, I can't even take my grandkid to a ball game in this city. The team moved down to the States a few years back.

Although I learned a lot about baseball that year, I learned much more from Jackie Robinson. I learned about how tough it is to be different, and how hard it is to be the one trying to make a change when everyone, it seems, is against you. I learned about turning the other cheek and not fighting back. I learned about believing in what you're doing. Most of all, I learned that all people are equal, no matter what the colour of their skin.

I try to remember those lessons in everything I do.

Thank you, Jackie Robinson.

So long, and *au revoir*.

# Acknowledgements

To Rob, Callum, and Tristan—you are the best thing that ever happened to me.

To my mom, who has always been my first and most enthusiastic reader. She travels North America, turning my books cover out on the shelves! Go, Baba Coach, Go! And to my dad, who loved to talk sports.

To my friend Marlene Cairns, who proves all things are possible. To Papa Ahearn, our "family" on the Ottawa River, my beloved high school friends from Winnipeg, the MacLeans, and the Russells. You always give me incredible support. Thanks also to my colleagues at CBC Radio on Prince Edward Island and all those avid readers at Glen Stewart Elementary.

Thanks to Linda Pruessen, who finally got her baseball book! And to Jordan Fenn, for taking my books to an even larger audience.

Writing a historical novel required lots of help. Thanks to Ron Kaulbach and Bob Williams for memories of Montreal, and to Bob Gray for baseball advice. This book was inspired by a CBC Radio documentary I co-produced in 1994 called "Field of Broken Dreams." I am indebted to everyone involved in that project, which won a Gold Medal at the New York Festival of Radio.